Ken leaned over, rubbing her arm with his hand. "Stay with me, Livvy," he urged. "You've got to hang in there until Winston and Maria can make it back with a rescue team."

Olivia shook her head almost imperceptibly. "Ken—"

"No!" he cried, one hand cradling the side of her face. "We can't give up hope."

Olivia smiled and kissed the palm of his hand. "Have I mentioned how much I love you?" she asked him, the words rasping in her throat like sandpaper.

"Not half as much as I love you," he replied. "I won't leave you, Livvy, no matter what happens."

Olivia gazed up into Ken's eyes, so full of pain and grief. In them, she saw the realization he couldn't bring himself to admit. He might not want to leave her. But if help didn't arrive soon, she might have to leave him. Forever.

Visit the Official Sweet Valley Web Site on the Internet at:

http://www.sweetvalley.com

EARTHQUAKE

Written by
Kate William

Created by
FRANCINE PASCAL

BANTAM BOOKS
NEW YORK · TORONTO · LONDON · SYDNEY · AUCKLAND

RL 6, age 12 and up

EARTHQUAKE

A Bantam Book / November 1998

Sweet Valley High® is a registered trademark of Francine Pascal.
Conceived by Francine Pascal.
Produced by 17th Street Productions,
a division of Daniel Weiss Associates, Inc.
33 West 17th Street
New York, NY 10011.
Cover photography by Michael Segal.

ISBN: 0-553-57024-2

Published simultaneously in the United States and Canada

Bantam Books are published by Bantam Books, a division of Bantam
Doubleday Dell Publishing Group, Inc. Its trademark, consisting of the
words "Bantam Books" and the portrayal of a rooster, is Registered in U.S.
Patent and Trademark Office and in other countries. Marca Registrada.
Bantam Books, 1540 Broadway, New York, New York 10036.

PRINTED IN THE UNITED STATES OF AMERICA

OPM   0 9 8 7 6 5 4 3 2 1

To Nicole Pascal Johansson

EARTHQUAKE

Chapter 1

"Don't die on me, Jessica. Please! Just stay with me!"

With you. I'm going to stay . . . Christian? Ken? Sam? Stay with—

"Come on, Jess. Please wake up!"

I can't wake up. I can't. Don't make me—

"Jess!"

Jessica Wakefield's face was wet. She reached up to wipe it dry, but her hand was wet too. She wondered how she'd gotten soaked and why her eyelids felt too heavy to open. She'd been asleep, she realized groggily. But that didn't make any sense. Why would she be sleeping during her own birthday party? She didn't remember going upstairs to bed.

1

The party. Practically every person in the junior class was there, along with a few seniors. Final exams were next week, and then graduation. She drifted into visions of her own graduation a year from now. She and Elizabeth were in their caps and gowns, with her best friend, Lila, complaining that the mortarboard cap would flatten her hairstyle. Jessica hoped the big, loose gown wouldn't make her look fat. Elizabeth would never worry about something like that. Elizabeth, unlike Jessica and Lila, hated spending a lot of time and energy on her hair and clothes and makeup.

"Why am I thinking about this?" Jessica murmured aloud. Surely there was something else she should be thinking about. Something totally crucial that had slipped her mind.

"Jessica?" asked a frantic male voice, close by. "Answer me, Jess!"

Who was that? Why was it was so hard to remember? She tried to move, and a strong band tightened across her chest. A dream, she decided. That was why she couldn't move, why she couldn't make sense of what was happening. This was all a crazy, mixed-up dream.

"Wake up, Jess!" said the voice. The hand on her arm felt familiar.

"Sam?" she asked. Sam Woodruff had been her boyfriend, the love of her life. She imagined his thick blond hair and quick grin, remembered his wacky sense of humor and his love for dirt-bike racing.

Something in her brain clicked on, and Jessica's heart plummeted to her stomach. The voice couldn't be Sam's, she remembered. Sam had died months ago, in a Jeep accident that she knew was no dream.

A Jeep accident.

More recent images flooded Jessica's brain. She remembered leaving her birthday party in her brand-new Jeep, remembered the road quivering beneath the tires as she sped through Sweet Valley's business district. Remembered hurtling forward, out of control, straight toward a telephone pole.

Jessica wrenched her eyes open. A boy's face hovered over her, its edges soft and blurry. She blinked, and the world slowly came into focus. She was slumped in the driver's seat of her new Jeep, the shoulder strap tight across her body. Her brother leaned over her, his face pale. Blood speckled his shirt.

"Steven," she said. Her voice was weaker than she'd expected.

"I couldn't wake you up," he said. "I was scared to death."

"Wh-What happened?"

"There was an earthquake, remember? You lost control of the Jeep. We rammed into a telephone pole."

Jessica shuddered, her mind flashing once again on the Jeep's headlong rush. She swallowed. There was no reason to be afraid now. The accident was over. But what was that strange wetness on her face?

"Steven! I'm bleeding! I'm bleeding!" she cried, frantically touching her cheeks. Her fingertips came away red and sticky.

Steven reached out and grabbed her wrists. "Jessica, you're OK. We're both scratched up, but it's nothing serious. Just a couple of shallow cuts. It was the fact that you were out cold that was scaring me."

"Swear?" she asked hopefully.

"I promise," he said, staring directly into her eyes.

Jessica's confidence began to return. "How long was I zoned out?"

"You've been unconscious for five or six minutes," her brother replied. "I didn't know what to do. I thought if you didn't wake up soon and I didn't find help . . ." Tears shone in his eyes, and the sight of them was almost more than Jessica could take. Her big brother never cried.

4

Jessica's head hurt, but she grinned weakly so that Steven would know she was all right. "I told you to take premed courses instead of prelaw," she said. She took a deep, shuddering breath. "But it's cool. We're both cool." She unfastened her seat belt and suddenly began to notice the Jeep's condition.

Chips of glass littered the front seats. The windshield was shattered, a spiderweb of cracks spreading out from its center. The hood had buckled. And part of the front bumper was bent around the scarred wooden telephone pole. "Oh, God, no!" she wailed. A dull pain sliced through her forehead at the force of her own cry, and she winced.

Steven grabbed her shoulders. "Jessica, what is it? Are you hurt?"

"Not me. The Jeep!" she sobbed. She'd been so psyched a few hours earlier, when their parents had presented her and Elizabeth with the keys. "It's only the first time I've driven my brand-new Wrangler, and it's ruined!"

Steven suddenly whirled on her. "Get over it. We have bigger things to worry about."

He gestured out the window, and Jessica felt her face go white. Suddenly she noticed the whine of sirens in the distance. The streetlights were dead, but the Jeep's headlamps illuminated her immediate surroundings. The road was churned up like the school football field after a game in the rain, with chunks of concrete jumbled together like trampled mud. Across the street, a Volvo lay on its side, its headlights shooting beams of white light in crazy directions.

Jessica gasped, stunned. A dented Jeep was nothing. She and Steven were lucky just to be alive.

Alive. Jessica sat bolt upright. "We have to get home!" she cried. "What about Elizabeth? What about Mom and Dad—they must be on their way back to the house. What about Lila and everyone else at my party?"

"What about Billie?" Steven added, his brown eyes terrified. Until that moment Jessica had forgotten about her brother's girlfriend, who had gone to the store and been stranded when Steven's old Volkswagen broke down. She and Steven had been on their way to pick her up. Panic squeezed Jessica's heart. They might have already lost everyone and everything they loved in the world.

Well, almost everyone, she thought, squeezing Steven's hand. Thank goodness she and her brother were here together. She hugged him again, tears streaming down her cheeks. "Liz has to be OK. She just has to."

"Can't you tell?" Steven asked, biting his lower lip as he searched her face.

It was clear that he believed Jessica really would know if Elizabeth was safe. The girls' brother often made fun of Jessica and Elizabeth's "twin sense," as the family called the sometimes uncanny ability of each twin to sense when the other was in danger. Jessica knew he'd seen it work often enough to accept its existence, even if his rational, prelaw brain couldn't explain it.

"Are you getting anything from her?" Steven pressed.

Jessica glared at him, crossing her arms in front of her. "It's not like a psychic telephone hot line I can dial up whenever I want to!"

Despite her denial, she tried to clear her mind and reach out toward her sister. If Elizabeth was in danger, the terror usually washed over Jessica in waves, with no warning. That's the way it had happened early in the school year, when the girls were candy stripers at Fowler Memorial and a hospital employee kidnapped Elizabeth. An eerie shiver of fear had prickled Jessica's spine, a fear that had nothing to do with her own situation—since, in

7

fact, Jessica was at a party at the time, perfectly safe and too intent on flirting with a good-looking guy to pay heed to her internal warning bells. Eventually Elizabeth had been rescued, unharmed. But Jessica would never forgive herself for having ignored her sisterly instincts when Elizabeth needed her.

Jessica knew she'd never make that mistake again. She searched her mind for any twinge of fear from her sister. But this time she felt only her own dread.

She turned away from Steven. "I don't sense anything," she said hopelessly, her voice quavering. Not feeling anything at all from Elizabeth right now was even more frightening than picking up on her twin's panic or pain.

"That's a good sign, right?" Steven asked.

"Yes, it's totally good," Jessica lied quickly, hoping to calm him. She nodded, but she couldn't meet his eyes. "I bet I don't feel anything from her because I'm too freaked myself."

"That must be it," Steven agreed. "Elizabeth's fine."

"If Liz was hurt or terrified . . . or worse . . . I'd know it," Jessica said, clenching her hands together to keep them from shaking. "Of course I would know."

But inside, she wasn't so sure.

The flagstone patio shivered against her face like a living creature, moist and cold. This time the trembling lasted only a few seconds. When it stopped, Elizabeth Wakefield raised her head to peer into the warm, smoke-filled night. She drew a deep breath, and her mouth filled with dust, the scent of chlorine, and the metallic tang of blood. She choked, coughing, before she forced her lungs to work normally.

"OK. I'm OK," she whispered hoarsely, desperate to convince herself.

The initial earthquake had plunged Elizabeth's birthday party into chaos just minutes earlier, but it seemed as if it had been an eternity since the ground was stable. Elizabeth had lived in southern California for all of her seventeen years—long enough to know she could expect aftershocks, possibly some as violent as the first quake. But for now the ground lay silent.

As her brain began to clear, Elizabeth took a quick inventory of her body. Her black jeans and fuchsia blouse clung to her skin, wet from being splashed by a wall of water that had leaped from the swimming pool when the ground began to rock.

She had bitten her lip, which accounted for the taste of blood in her mouth. Her forehead was bleeding too—a trickle ran down her face from a shallow cut above her left eyebrow. She wiped at it with her hand and winced at the sting. A head wound. Had she been unconscious? She didn't know for sure.

She felt dazed and stupid, as if she'd just woken from a troubled sleep. But she wasn't dizzy, and her head ached no worse than the rest of her body, which was bruised and sore from Elizabeth's having thrown herself facedown onto the patio when the earthquake struck. She remembered that moment, remembered pulling Devon Whitelaw down beside her, her arm slung protectively over his back.

"Devon!" Elizabeth twisted around and found him, still lying next to her near the barbecue grill. She reached out and touched him gingerly. Though the patio had stopped shaking, his body trembled under her hand. She squeezed his shoulder and felt goose bumps rising beneath the damp cotton of his T-shirt. "Are you all right?" she asked, her voice a hoarse whisper. She coughed, trying to clear her throat of acrid dust. Devon moaned.

Unlike Elizabeth and the rest of her friends, Devon hadn't lived in California for very long. He'd recently moved to Sweet Valley from the East Coast and had never been through even a minor earthquake, except for a small tremor earlier that day.

"Come on, Devon. Talk to me." Elizabeth sat up and skimmed Devon's arms and legs with her fingers, as she'd learned in first-aid class. She felt no broken bones, saw no blood or other signs of injury. She checked the slate blue eyes that had captivated so many girls and saw that his pupils were not dilated; his thick, light brown hair masked no apparent swellings. But still he hadn't spoken. Maybe he was in shock.

"Devon, are you hurt?" she asked again, her voice rising.

Devon shook his head and opened his mouth as if to reply, but he only moaned again. He wasn't injured, Elizabeth decided. Just terrified.

Elizabeth blinked a few times and looked around. Suddenly their surroundings—her family's dimly lit backyard, still hazy with smoke and dust—snapped into focus. The house on Calico Drive had always been her home, but the scene now seemed as foreign as the surface of the moon.

The electricity had gone out a few minutes before, leaving the nightmarish landscape illuminated dimly by an ominous orange glow in the sky and by the few garden lanterns whose votive candles had remained lit against all odds. The far side of the patio had cracked and buckled, the flagstones torn and furrowed like dirt in a freshly plowed field. All around Elizabeth, cries and groans punctuated a cacophony of creaks and crashes from the direction of the house, which was invisible through the smoke-filled night. Most of the people she cared about huddled on the patio or lay motionless on the lawn.

The people she cared about.

Elizabeth leaped to her feet, ignoring the sudden jab of pain in her head. "Jessica!" she screamed, staring wildly around her for a glimpse of the golden hair and slender form of her identical twin sister. She took a few shaky steps, and the patio quivered beneath her. For a split second she wondered how her light footfalls could shake a stone patio.

"No!" Devon screamed, burying his face in his arms.

It's just another aftershock, Elizabeth told herself,

a mild one. The shaking subsided within seconds, and Elizabeth choked back panic. Where was Jessica? What about her parents and her older brother, Steven?

"Jessica!" she called again. Then she remembered. Jessica and Steven had driven the twins' new Jeep into town to pick up his girlfriend, Billie. OK. It was all coming back to her. She took a deep breath to calm her racing heart.

Her parents were away from the house too, Elizabeth reminded herself. They'd left the party early to go to the movies, leaving Steven and Billie as chaperons. Elizabeth blinked back tears. She had no idea how bad the damage was in any other part of Sweet Valley. She had no way of contacting her family or even of knowing if they were alive.

She pushed that thought out of her mind. "Wherever they are, it has to be better than this," she whispered, gazing in disbelief at the chaos around her. Friends she'd known her entire life were struggling to their feet, sobbing and wild-eyed, nursing wounds, or silently picking through the rubble like refugees in a war zone.

She had to figure out what to do. There were people that needed aid. Elizabeth looked at her former boyfriend, Devon, hoping he'd snapped out of his stupor and was ready to help her. But the normally able and quick-witted Devon was still lying on the ground, his eyes squeezed shut and his legs curled up in front of him.

It seemed as if Elizabeth was on her own.

Chapter 2

Ken Matthews stumbled through the darkness of the Wakefields' ruined kitchen, coughing and gasping from the smoke and dust that filled the air. He hadn't felt this clumsy and helpless since last fall, when a car accident had left him temporarily blind. He'd feared then that he would never see again—and never play football again—but his vision had returned before the season ended, and he'd resumed his place in the starting lineup. Football and other sports had once again become the most important thing in Ken's life—until the day he met a sensitive, poetic girl named Freeverse in an Internet chat room.

"Olivia!" he hollered. "Where are you?"

He and Olivia had fallen in love on-line but for

weeks had known each other only by their screen names, Quarter and Freeverse. When they'd finally met in person, he'd been disappointed to learn that Freeverse was only Olivia Davidson, a girl he'd known since kindergarten without ever really knowing her. He'd always thought she was a flaky artist, and she'd assumed he was a dumb jock. But when they decided to give their relationship a shot despite their differences, he'd made the best decision of his life.

Ken tossed aside a chair and stumbled on some broken glass. He grappled with the countertop to keep himself from falling on the shards. "Livvy! Please answer me!" he cried.

He couldn't believe any of this was happening. Ten minutes earlier he and Olivia had been chatting away, blissfully happy to have settled their differences after an argument that had lasted for nearly two weeks. The familiar kitchen had been spacious and cheerful, with its bright lights and exposed oak ceiling beams. Strains of music and laughter filtered in from the backyard, and Olivia's hazel eyes looked almost green, reflecting the colors of a flowery abstract print on her dress. Her wild brown curls framed her round face, and her lips still shone softly from his last kiss.

Now, as he searched for a glimpse of her, he wondered if he'd been transported to some science-fiction hellhole. The electric lights were out, but a few dull orange flames now flickered at the far end of the room, casting eerie shadows over crumbling walls, splintered furniture, and crushed appliances. Nothing else moved.

The most frightening part was that he was all alone. He had tried to keep hold of Olivia's hand, but they'd been separated in the earthquake. Now he couldn't find her anywhere, couldn't find any of their classmates who'd been in the kitchen with them when the ground began to shake. Part of the house had caved in, and the walls that remained standing emitted a constant chorus of creaks and groans that made it hard for Ken to hear anything else, hard for him to concentrate on listening for a cry or a moan from Olivia or the others.

"Can anybody hear me?" he yelled. "Olivia!" He had to find her. He just had to. They had been together for only a short time, but already he couldn't imagine life without her.

"Olivia!" he called, his throat already sore from breathing the pungent smoke and from yelling her name. A quick aftershock rumbled the floor beneath him. Suddenly the room around him exploded in a torrent of sound and motion. Chunks of plaster rained down around him.

Ken covered his head with his arms and rode it out. When the shaking stopped, he realized he was standing in front of what had been a hip-high bank of cabinets topped by a tiled counter. A jumble of drywall, metal ductwork, and electrical wiring had fallen from the ceiling, nearly obscuring the counter beneath it. The end of a thick wooden ceiling beam jutted out from the center of the pile, its other end buried in a pile of debris that covered much of the floor beyond the countertop.

Ken's mind flashed back to the earthquake, back to a moment he'd managed not to think about. In agonizing slow motion, he saw Olivia in the darkness, raising her slender arms in a futile effort to protect herself. He saw her terror-filled eyes as the heavy oak beam crashed down. He'd tried to run, tried to reach her in time, but there was too much debris in the way. Olivia had disappeared in a rain of drywall, her scream cut short. He'd lost her position in the succeeding aftershocks, had gotten turned around by the dark and confusion.

But this was the same wooden ceiling beam

that had fallen on her. Ken was sure of it. That meant Olivia was somewhere beyond the counter, probably lying helpless in the debris of the caved-in ceiling, just under that beam. A shower of sparks erupted from some wires nearby. For a moment the sparks illuminated a small, delicate object sticking out of the pile. It was the soft, heartbreaking shape of a shoe, one of the balletlike slippers that Olivia favored. Ken's stomach shifted dangerously, bile rising in his throat.

"Olivia!" he screamed, his eyes desperately trained on the ceiling beam as he prayed that the next flash of light would reveal some movement. "Livvy, can you hear me?"

He couldn't get to her. The row of cabinets blocked his path, and the debris from the ceiling was too unstable to climb over. He'd have to move the chunks of wood, metal, and drywall, one by one, until he reached her.

"No, no, no, please, no . . ." A girl was sobbing, her terrified tone echoing the fear and confusion in Elizabeth's heart. Elizabeth focused on the voice. She couldn't help her family right now, but there were people all around her who were bewildered, lost, and terrified.

She squeezed her eyes shut for a moment, trying to steel herself against despair. She knew she'd be a lot braver with her sister, Jessica, at her side. Jessica was usually the life of the party, flirting her way from one guy to the next without a second thought. But when it came to emergency situations, Jessica always displayed a brave, rational side that never ceased to amaze Elizabeth. Normally the organized, responsible one, Elizabeth often found that she needed her sister as a rock to lean on in times of trouble. Elizabeth could always come up with a plan, but it took Jessica's guts to carry it out.

Their strengths complemented one another. It was their differences that made them an unbeatable team.

But Jessica wasn't here. A wave of loneliness swept over Elizabeth, and she tried not to let it consume her. *Keep calm, Liz. You have to find your friends and make sure they're all right. Somebody has to take control.* Elizabeth clenched her fists and looked around the patio area.

Her gaze fell on Caroline Pearce, who sat shivering by the edge of the pool, staring in confusion at part of an uprooted tree that lay on the flagstones beside her. Her pink dress clung wetly to her slender form, making her look as small and frail as a child. Elizabeth crouched at her side.

"Caroline, are you hurt?" she asked.

Caroline shook her head slowly, her dusty red curls reflecting glints of light from a nearby lantern.

"Caroline, it's me, Elizabeth. You have to pull yourself together. A lot of people need our help."

The redheaded girl stared at Elizabeth, and her eyes seemed to clear. Then she closed her mouth, nodded, and took a few deep breaths.

"I'm OK," Caroline said, her voice cracking. "It's Ronnie. He's—" Caroline broke off, gesturing limply at the tree.

Elizabeth's heart leaped into her throat. Slowly she turned to look at the fallen cedar. What she saw made her blood run cold. A lifeless body lay broken and battered underneath its branches.

"Ronnie Edwards?" Elizabeth whispered, tears springing to her eyes. "Is he . . . ?"

"I don't know, Liz. I can't—" Caroline sobbed, and started rocking forward, holding her arm across her stomach and one hand over her mouth.

Elizabeth stood on shaky legs. She walked around the tree and saw his face—a face she'd known forever—white and chalky beneath the emerald green leaves. His skin practically shone in the darkness. Moving as if through molasses, Elizabeth crouched down and found his wrist. She held her breath. There was no pulse.

"No!" Elizabeth cried with a whimper. Caroline's sobs grew louder as if in reply. "He can't be . . ." Elizabeth gasped for breath and turned away. She and Ronnie had never been exactly close, but he had dated her best friend, Enid, for a time, and he was so young. He'd had his whole future ahead of him. Elizabeth's entire body ached with despair.

Someone stumbled into her side, and Elizabeth had to grab a tree branch to keep herself from tumbling over. It was Amy Sutton, her straight blond hair streaked with dirt. Her eyes were wide with terror. Elizabeth rose, pulling Amy up with her. She turned Amy away so that the obviously stricken girl wouldn't have to see Ronnie's body.

Amy clutched at Elizabeth as Caroline rose to stand beside them, breathing slowly to calm her sobs.

"Barry? Have you seen him?" Amy demanded. "He was right next to me, but now I can't find him. God, Liz, what happened to him?"

Elizabeth glanced around but didn't see Amy's boyfriend, Barry Rork, among the people in the large backyard. Ronnie was dead. Barry could be dead too. Any of her friends could be gone forever, but Elizabeth knew she couldn't think that way. It would only make her feel even more helpless.

"Amy, listen to me," Elizabeth said, the steadiness of her voice surprising her. "We can't let ourselves panic. We have to stay calm."

"Stay calm," Caroline repeated, tears streaming down her face. She was still shaking.

Amy shook her head. "Oh, my gosh! Liz, what about my mother? What if my house—" She burst into explosive sobs. Elizabeth knew what Amy was feeling. The Suttons lived only four blocks away. If there was this much damage at the Wakefields', the Sutton house might be a wreck too.

"Amy, try to focus," Elizabeth coaxed her gently.

A.J. Morgan appeared through the smoke. His shirt was ripped, but he seemed unhurt. Elizabeth breathed a ragged sigh of relief. Amy and Caroline were both known to be excitable, but A.J. had always been steady and dependable.

"A.J., have you seen Barry?" Elizabeth asked, hoping to quiet Amy's hysterics.

"Yeah, back there," A.J. said vaguely, pointing. "He looked OK to me," he added, noticing Amy.

"Good. See, Amy, he's fine. Why don't you go try to find him?" Elizabeth said.

Relief spread over Amy's face, and she was off and running. She disappeared into the darkness before Elizabeth was even through speaking.

Elizabeth looked at A.J. and Caroline. "OK, you guys—"

"I saw Wilkins just before it struck," A.J. interrupted, touching the back of his neck as if he were checking to make sure he wasn't bleeding. "He was heading toward the house."

Elizabeth gasped. "Todd?" she managed weakly. She turned to look at her house and felt her knees go weak. The roof had collapsed, and one side of the house looked as if it had been crushed underneath a giant's heel. If Todd was inside, the chances that he was OK, let alone alive, were slim.

Elizabeth struggled to steady herself. Aside from a couple of breakups, Todd had been Elizabeth's boyfriend for a whole year—until Devon moved to town and forced her into one of the most painful decisions of her life. She'd broken up with Todd to be with Devon, and for weeks Todd was too hurt even to speak to her. But tonight, less than an hour earlier, they'd finally talked and set things straight between them. Elizabeth didn't know if she and Todd would ever date again, but at least they'd parted on friendly terms.

Despite the tension between them lately, Elizabeth had never stopped loving Todd. Now she wondered if she'd ever have the chance to tell him so. She felt her resolve to be brave start to crumble.

"Was anyone else in the house?" Caroline asked A.J.

He covered his face with his hands. "I don't know!"

"Enid and Maria?" Elizabeth asked weakly.

"I don't know!" A.J. repeated, his voice muffled.

"We'll get everyone to safety," Elizabeth said with more certainty than she felt. After seeing Ronnie, she was hanging on to hope by a very slim thread. "If we all work together . . ."

"We can't do anything for them! We have to get out of here before it starts up again!" A.J. cried, his eyes wild. "Half your house is in splinters, Liz. The rest could go in the next aftershock. We should move farther from the building."

Elizabeth choked back a sick feeling of dread. Wasn't anyone even going to try to remain calm? Maybe if she gave them some direction, they would be more likely to help.

"Here's the plan," Elizabeth said, grabbing

A.J.'s wrist. "A.J., you help me start moving people away from the house. Caroline, check that group near the bandstand. Find out how many people are hurt—"

A small section of the Wakefields' roof broke apart and tumbled to the ground, sending up a loud clatter and a new cloud of dust. A.J. yelped at the sound. Then he broke free from Elizabeth's grasp and ran into the darkness, moving farther from the house.

Caroline doubled over, coughing, and Elizabeth realized the smoke was becoming thicker. It was billowing through the trees that blocked her view of the house next door. Orange flames flickered behind black branches. The house next door was on fire. Elizabeth wrenched her horrified gaze away from the blaze.

"That leaves only the two of us," she said, struggling to keep her voice steady. "Caroline, you and I will split up. See who you can find. I'm going closer to the house. People might be trapped." She ignored the question of which people that might be. Then the ground trembled, interrupting her instructions.

Caroline screamed and fell to her knees. Elizabeth braced her legs to ride out the motion.

The aftershock lasted only a few seconds, but another series of creaks and rumblings spilled into the air from the direction of the Wakefield house.

Four of their classmates materialized out of the smoke, swerving around Elizabeth and Caroline in their race to get away from the house. Elizabeth couldn't tell who they were. The smoke was too thick, and their clothes and hair were too caked with dirt to be recognizable.

"Stop!" Elizabeth yelled after them, her throat scratchy. "We need help here!" They didn't even slow down. "Get up, Caroline," she urged. "Please!"

The red-haired girl shook her head weakly. "I can't," she whimpered. "It's too much."

Blood was dripping down her own face again, and Elizabeth scrubbed it away with her hand. It was no use. She couldn't even stop her own shallow cut from bleeding. How could she possibly hope to stop the nightmare that raged around her? She wanted to run away, like the others. Or just sink to the ground, like Caroline and Devon, and hide her face in her hands.

Maybe Caroline was right. Maybe it was just too much to handle.

✿   ✿   ✿

Devon covered his ears with his hands, trying to block the hideous sounds that assaulted him from all directions—screams, sobs, distant sirens, and the crunch of wood and metal. This wasn't happening. It couldn't be. The earth was solid. It wasn't supposed to betray him by moving and groaning beneath his feet as if it were alive. He wished desperately that he'd stayed on the East Coast, where the earth knew its place. Where walls stayed vertical, water rested quietly in swimming pools, and chimneys weren't uprooted like saplings and hurled through roofs.

Devon had always prided himself on staying in control, on projecting an image of utter coolness. Now, for the first time in his life, he felt totally vulnerable, at the mercy of an enormous power he couldn't control and didn't understand.

The earthquake had been terrifying in its suddenness, but at least he hadn't had time to anticipate it—to fear it. Now the ground was still, but he was even more frightened. He couldn't think straight, didn't know what to do. The aftershocks would keep coming, one after another, like predators who traveled in a pack, hunting him down. And there wasn't a thing he could do to stop them.

Let Elizabeth be brave, he told himself. From the looks of things, she was the only one. She was yelling for people to help care for the injured, to search for survivors in the wreckage—all the things people did in the last half hour of disaster movies. But nobody paid attention to her.

Bruce Patman sprinted off around the side of the house, mumbling something about getting home to his parents. Tall, sophisticated Cheryl Thomas wandered past, calling out for her stepsister, Annie Whitman, as tears dripped down her face.

Other people were crying, screaming, or praying out loud. But the most terrifying of all were those who lay still and silent.

Devon wondered how Elizabeth could stand there grimly trying to organize rescue efforts when everything she owned had just been destroyed. He felt a twinge of guilt for letting her handle the load herself but blocked it out.

Even before his parents had died, they'd never made time for him. Devon had taken care of himself, even as a child. Now he was an orphan, and he'd learned through painful experience that the only person he could trust was himself. Before he worried about anyone else, he would look out for number one.

Why should he risk his own life by searching through the precarious wreckage? He barely knew most of these kids. They weren't his responsibility.

No, I'm going to stay exactly where I am, Devon decided. Later he might make his way to the street, jump on his motorcycle, and speed away from the smoke, the blood, and the destruction. He pulled his knees closer to his chest and squeezed his eyes shut, wishing the world around him would just fade away.

Chapter 3

"This is all your fault!" Lila Fowler shouted.

Todd Wilkins rolled his eyes. "An earthquake is my fault? Right. And for my next trick, I'll create a nice solar eclipse. How is this my fault?"

"Not the earthquake, jock brain," Lila said, flipping back her light brown hair. "The two of us being stuck in this hole together." She gestured around the room with one perfectly manicured hand. "If you had waited your turn for the bathroom instead of barging in while I was innocently fixing my makeup—"

"Then you'd be trapped in here alone, and I'd be out in the hallway listening to walls collapsing instead of listening to your yapping," he shot back. "Believe me, if I had my choice—"

31

"Your choice? Do you think I want to be here with you?" she demanded.

"You're damn lucky to be here with me," he said. "Who saved your precious face from getting torn up by flying glass a few minutes ago?"

"Try the door again," she ordered.

"Try it yourself," he said. "What am I, your slave?"

Lila stared at him expectantly, her eyebrows raised.

Of all the people attending the twins' birthday party, rich, spoiled Lila Fowler was the last one Todd would have chosen to be trapped with. Yet here he was, huddled in the dim, downstairs bathroom with one of his least favorite people, taking orders on top of everything else.

He desperately wished Lila had sustained an injury—preferably a sprained tongue.

Todd took a deep breath and replied in a quiet, controlled voice. "Lila, the door was stuck shut when I tried it five minutes ago. Do you think the door fairy came along and waved a magic wand at it?"

"Well, I haven't heard you come up with any brilliant ideas."

"If you could keep your mouth shut for a minute, maybe I'd be able to think of a plan."

Lila fished through her purse and pulled out a book of matches.

"Uh, Lila, aren't you forgetting something? You don't smoke."

She glared at him and then stood to relight the decorative candle that sat on the back of the toilet tank. "Let there be light," she said regally before rejoining him in the corner. Suddenly the room was bathed in a honey-colored glow. Todd hated to admit that Lila had come up with a good idea, but the light was reassuring.

At least it was until a mild aftershock shook the room. Lila gripped Todd's arm. He timed the tremor on his watch. Six seconds. It was the shortest one yet. He thought the intervals between aftershocks were getting longer as well. Maybe the worst was over. Maybe the earth was finally settling down to rest.

The tile floor stopped rocking beneath them, but a slight metallic ringing echoed through the room for a few seconds. Lila pointed at the light fixture over the sink. It was still vibrating. As they watched, it slipped from the wall and crashed to the floor. A shower of glass chips skidded around the room. Lila yelped, and Todd instinctively shielded her with his arms.

A moment later Lila pulled away and crossed her arms in front of her, blushing. Todd knew Lila prided herself on being in control of her emotions at all times. She was clearly embarrassed to have him see how freaked she was. *No doubt she'll never forgive me for it,* he thought wryly.

"What about the window?" she asked. Her voice was as icy as ever, but he saw that her eyes were moist.

He shook his head and pretended not to notice that she was on the verge of tears. "That fallen tree still has it blocked," he replied, nodding toward the window. "We'd never be able to squeeze around it."

"Someone will rescue us soon," Lila said in her most confident, rich-girl voice. She rubbed at an imaginary spot on her formfitting black pants. "I don't know about you, but they'll obviously miss *me.*"

Todd bit his lip. "I wouldn't count on it," he said slowly. "From the sounds of those crashes we heard earlier, there's been big-time damage to the rest of the house. I bet other people need help a lot worse than we do."

Todd's thoughts immediately turned to Elizabeth, and his heart twisted in fear. He'd last seen her a few minutes before the earthquake struck. He'd turned for one last look before he walked into the house. She was on the back patio, wearing a deep pink blouse as she flipped barbecued chicken on the grill. The reflected lights of the garden lanterns played in her golden hair as she talked with Enid Rollins.

Todd felt as if he'd been in love with Elizabeth all his life. Then Devon Whitelaw had moved to town, and everything changed. Devon was handsome and brilliant and dangerous, and every girl in school seemed to fall for him, to the disgust of Todd and most of his male friends. He'd trusted Elizabeth, but she'd fallen under Devon's spell as well. And in the end Elizabeth was the only girl Devon wanted.

She'd accepted a date to the prom with Devon but then couldn't choose between the two of them. She'd spent the entire night dancing with Todd while Jessica impersonated Elizabeth with Devon. The kicker was, Elizabeth had allowed Jessica to do it—had known about it all along.

Ever since that night Todd had felt as if he were wading through quicksand. He couldn't concentrate on basketball, or on his friends, or on studying for next week's final exams. He suddenly didn't care about yearbooks or awards ceremonies or summer plans. He had no interest in any of the end-of-year hoopla that usually made June the most exciting month at Sweet Valley High. Without Elizabeth, none of it seemed to matter. All his plans had crumbled to dust.

He'd almost stayed home from the twins' birthday party that night. He didn't think he could stand to see Elizabeth, and for once in his life he wasn't up for a party. Then he'd received his acceptance to a summer basketball program in North Carolina, which would free him from having to face Elizabeth all summer, and suddenly he'd changed his mind about coming to the birthday party. He'd told Elizabeth he was leaving for the summer, and they'd wished each other well and meant it. Todd felt his eyes moisten with tears. What if Elizabeth was hurt . . . or worse? What if that was the last conversation they would ever have?

Another aftershock rocked the house, and Todd felt the walls shift. Lila buried her head against his chest, and he held her tightly, realizing for the first time that they might actually die. A crack split one wall with a report like a gunshot.

Lila's body shuddered, and Todd closed his eyes.

The worst thing was the uncertainty. He didn't know how bad the damage was in the rest of the house, or whether the bathroom walls were about to tumble down around them. And he didn't know if Elizabeth was alive and unharmed.

Todd couldn't bear to think of how frightened Elizabeth would be, alone in the middle of an earthquake. He longed to wrap his arms around her, imagined the scent of her hair and the curve of her back against his hands.

But it was Lila whom he cradled against his chest, Lila whose lemon-scented hair he smelled. Lila, who was even more self-centered and superficial than Jessica. It was no surprise that the two girls were best friends.

The room was still. He glanced around furtively, trying to determine how bad the damage was. The walls were still standing, but a long, dark crack ran horizontally along one side of the room. It was a sure sign of structural damage.

Todd's heart pounded with fear. "Oh, no," he whispered.

The fire in the corner of the room was larger now. Ken could hear the flames crackling. But it didn't seem to be spreading in his direction at the moment, so Ken ignored it. Rescuing Olivia was the only thing that mattered. He shoved a splintered chair out of the way and dodged a jet of water that spurted from a burst pipe. Some metal ductwork still lay between him and the pile of debris where Olivia was buried.

"Olivia!" he shouted again. "Answer me, Livvy, please!" The only response was another soft fall of dust from the ceiling.

"She's unconscious," he said aloud. "That's why she isn't answering." He couldn't bring himself to consider the other possibility. All he had to do was push the metal ducts aside and somehow move the ceiling beam and broken sheets of drywall that covered her, and Olivia would wake up and throw her arms around him.

"Olivia!" he screamed in anguish.

A dog howled, and Ken jumped. He'd been hearing consistent barking in the background, but the sudden, high-pitched howl set his already fraying nerves on edge.

"Ken, is that you?" called a girl's voice. Ken's heart pounded in his chest. "We're under the kitchen table!" the voice continued. It wasn't Olivia. It was Maria Santelli, another junior from

38

school. Ken gulped, a flood of emotions washing over him. He was still frantic about Olivia, but other people he cared about were trapped in the rubble as well. It was good to hear a voice—any voice. And he was glad that Maria sounded OK. Maybe she could help him rescue Olivia from under the wreckage. Suddenly her words sank in. She'd said "we." Maybe he was wrong about Olivia being trapped under the ceiling beam. Maybe she was safe with Maria.

Ken couldn't see the sturdy kitchen table from where he stood, but he knew it was near what had once been a set of sliding glass doors that led to the patio—on the side of the kitchen that wasn't as badly damaged. "Maria, who's with you?" he called into the darkness. "Is Olivia there? Are you all right?"

"It's me and Annie Whitman," Maria yelled back. She and Annie were on the cheerleading squad at school. "I guess we were both out cold for a few minutes. I'm OK now. Annie broke her arm, and I think she hurt her head." The dog howled again. "Prince Albert's here too."

"I think Olivia's trapped under a pile of stuff," he called back to Maria, finally knocking aside the last piece of ductwork that separated him from the

39

oak beam and other debris. "She's still mostly covered up. She must be unconscious, probably hurt bad." He grabbed the end of the beam in both hands and yanked, but it didn't budge. "Maria, I can't get her out of here by myself. I need your help. Can you follow my voice?"

"It'll take me a minute to climb out from under here," Maria said. "The dishwasher's blocking my way."

"Hurry!" he yelled. He pulled a chunk of drywall from the pile and tossed it aside, uncovering Olivia's lower leg. Ken gasped. She'd been wearing black tights, but they were ash-gray and ripped to shreds. Her skin was dusty and cold to the touch. Ken couldn't tell if she was breathing, but he had to believe that she was. Anything else was unthinkable.

He heard a male voice coming from the direction of the table. "Egbert, is that you?" he called. Winston Egbert was Maria's boyfriend and a good friend of Ken's. "I need help over here!"

"I had to clear a path in here from the outside," Winston said. He sounded relieved but tense. "I've got Maria out from under the table. We'll be right there."

"Keep talking so we can find you, Ken," Maria suggested. "Have you reached Olivia?"

"I can only see her leg," Ken answered, trying to push down the panic that was rising in his throat. Prince Albert had stopped barking abruptly, and the absence of the familiar noise left Ken with a strange feeling of emptiness. He forced himself to keep speaking, to fill the void. "It's worse than I thought. The whole damn refrigerator is on top of her!"

Suddenly Winston wriggled into view with Maria close behind. Her dark eyes were frightened and her usually glossy brown hair was coated with dust, but she seemed calm.

"We left Annie under the table with Prince Albert," Maria explained in the take-charge voice she used when speaking at student council meetings. "She's kind of weak, but she'll be safe there until we can help her out of the house."

"What can I do?" Winston asked.

"We have to try to move this thing," Ken replied, gesturing at the huge beam.

Winston slapped his hands together. "Let's do it," he said.

He and Ken gripped the end of the wooden beam and threw their weight against it. There was a loud creak, and a large chunk of plaster fell from the ceiling. Ken and Winston both jumped back. The

41

last thing Ken wanted to do was make things worse.

Maria yelped, then covered her mouth with her hand. "Sorry," she said when she'd regained her composure. "Did it move at all?"

"A little," Ken said, squinting up at the ceiling. For a moment there he had thought the whole place was going to cave in. But from where he stood, it didn't seem as if the beam was holding anything up, and they had to move it to get to Olivia. They were going to have to chance it. "I think we can do this," he said.

Maria looked toward the back of the house. "Winston, what's going on outside?" she asked.

"People are injured, but I didn't see anything too horrible. At least it's not nearly as awful as it is in here," Winston said as the three of them jockeyed for position around the massive beam. "Was anyone else in the house?"

Ken shook his head. "Who knows?" he said. "Let's go." This time he and Winston tried to lift the beam with their shoulders while Maria leaned forward, ready to reach in and pull Olivia to safety. The beam refused to budge. Ken gasped for breath. He was rapidly approaching desperation.

"We have to get her out of there!" His voice was a near wail.

Winston was doubled over, bracing his hands above his knees. "Hey! What about Todd?" he asked, sucking wind. "Where did he go?"

An image of his best friend flashed through Ken's mind, and his stomach turned. "Oh, God," Ken said. "The last time I saw him, he was heading to the bathroom."

"Maybe I should go check on him," Maria suggested tentatively.

"No way. You're not going anywhere alone," Winston said, his mouth in a grim line. "We'll get Olivia out first, then check the house for other . . . survivors." For once, the class clown could find nothing to joke about. Even in the gloom, Ken could see how white his friend's face was beneath its sprinkling of freckles. Ken's own hands were trembling, but he tried to choke down his fear and concentrate on helping his girlfriend.

Another aftershock rumbled beneath them. Vibrations traveled up through the soles of Ken's feet, shaking him to his bones. A chorus of creaks and thuds rose from the walls around them. The three friends clutched one another.

As the earth's motion stopped, a weak, wordless cry sounded from the direction of the kitchen table. Prince Albert resumed his barking.

"Annie?" Winston called, gripping Maria's hand. He broke into a spasm of coughing.

"She needs us," Maria said softly, looking at Ken.

He swallowed hard, trying to keep himself from breaking down. "You should help her," he said in a tight voice. "We need more muscle power to help Olivia anyway."

Maria squeezed Ken's shoulder. "You stay here," she told him. "Winston and I will get Annie out of the house and then come back with more people to help Olivia."

Ken nodded. Maria was right, but he felt more hopeless every moment.

"We'll find a cell phone," Winston suggested. "Call the fire department."

"Good idea," Maria said. "Lila or Bruce ought to have one." Lila Fowler and Bruce Patman were from the richest families in town, and both liked to flaunt their status by carrying expensive gadgets. For once, Ken thought, their vanity might actually be useful—if Winston could find either of them in what was probably complete chaos in the backyard.

Maria and Winston skirted around the pile of rubble that still held Olivia. Ken watched as

44

Winston's back disappeared around a corner, and then he was alone.

Moments later an aftershock nearly wrenched the end of the oak beam from Ken's hands. The pile of rubble shifted, and he heard a whimper from beneath it.

"Olivia!" he yelled, horrified to know she was hurting, but relieved that she was alive.

As the tremor stilled, part of a bathroom sink was suddenly flung downward from what was left of the upstairs story. As it fell, it thudded against the beam, rocking the whole pile again. Olivia screamed.

The scream sliced through Ken's heart. He'd never heard a person in such anguish. And it was Olivia, his Freeverse. He couldn't bear it. Adrenaline coursed through Ken's body, and he grabbed the end of the beam once more. He leaned into it with his shoulder, ten times harder than he'd ever rushed an opposing linebacker for a touchdown. A hundred times harder. The beam finally gave and tumbled off the pile of rubble and off Olivia.

He rushed in to fling other bits of debris away from her slender form. Her skin shone ghostly white in the dark room, and her eyes were closed.

"Honey, it's Ken. Can you hear me?" She only moaned.

With the oak beam gone, Ken could see that the Wakefields' refrigerator lay on its side, its corner pinning Olivia's arm. Another beam, as heavy as the first, rested across the refrigerator. Ken choked back panic. He'd barely been able to move the first beam. How would he ever manage to free her?

Tears blurred his vision. He angrily rubbed them away before grabbing the corner of the refrigerator with both hands. It was crushing her arm. Moving it could injure her worse. But he had to risk it. There was no other way to get her out. He pushed against the refrigerator, rocking it slightly. Olivia screamed again, and Ken winced. A cloud of drywall dust erupted from the rubble, and he began to cough. This was no use. He slumped down beside her, taking her free hand in his. "I'm sorry. I don't want to hurt you," he said gently.

Olivia opened her eyes. They were wide and blank, and she didn't seem to see him at all. She didn't answer.

Ken had never felt so desperate. Every ounce of strength in his body wasn't enough to move the refrigerator and other debris off her. And even the slightest motion hurt her terribly. The girl he loved was in trouble, and all he could do was sit and wait for help. Tears streamed down Ken's face as he stroked her hair. "I'm here, Livvy," he told her. "I won't leave you. I love you."

Recognition dawned slowly in Olivia's wide eyes, and with it, pain. She gazed at him for a moment, then silently mouthed one word. "Ken."

Chapter 4

"Good old Mom!" Jessica called as she pulled a box out of the backseat. She twisted around, sat back down behind the steering wheel, and held up the box for Steven's inspection.

It was a first-aid kit. Steven managed a weak smile. "Of course. She probably bought that before she bought the Jeep, knowing the way you drive."

"Watch it, buddy," Jessica warned, opening an antiseptic wipe. "I was behind the wheel of this car and we lived, didn't we? Now hold still." She leaned forward and touched the wipe to a cut on Steven's cheek. He winced as the medicine stung the open wound.

"Oh, be a man," Jessica chided.

Steven leaned back in his seat and took a deep

breath as Jessica continued to clean him up. He'd been terrified just after the accident, when he couldn't wake his sister. Now he was beginning to breathe easier about her. Except for a bump on the head, she seemed almost like her usual self.

Watching over Jessica always came naturally to Steven. Of course, he was protective of Elizabeth too. But Elizabeth was usually so levelheaded and sensible. Jessica was the twin who got herself into ridiculous and sometimes dangerous situations.

It was Jessica who had joined Bruce Patman's thrill-seeking group, Club X, determined to prove she could do anything a boy could do. When she accepted the club's challenge to walk across a high, narrow railroad bridge, she'd nearly been killed by a speeding train. It was Jessica who'd been lured into a strange cult led by a charismatic stranger named Adam Marvel, who would have kidnapped her if Elizabeth and Sam hadn't arrived in time. Jessica was always falling in love with the wrong guy or jumping into risky situations without thinking. She was only four minutes younger than Elizabeth, but Steven always thought of Jessica as his youngest sister.

But now she was taking charge, and she seemed fine. He was worried about Elizabeth and his parents, too. But Elizabeth was at home, at a party with a hundred people. His folks had gone to the movies. He couldn't be sure they were safe, but at least they were together. Only one person he loved was alone and terrified, he thought. Billie.

"All done!" Jessica said, pressing a bandage against his forehead. She flipped down the vanity mirror and went to work on herself.

Steven had met Billie Winkler when she moved in with him, by accident, in his apartment just off the campus of Sweet Valley University. He'd assumed someone named Billie was a guy, and had been stunned to learn that his new roommate was a beautiful young woman with silky chestnut hair. Despite occasional misunderstandings, they'd been together ever since. And he'd grown to love her with an intensity that still astounded him at times. Billie was his heart, his whole life.

"She just has to be OK!"

He didn't realize he had whispered the words aloud until Jessica reached over and squeezed his hand. "She'll be fine," she assured him, but her smile was uncertain. "As soon as we get fixed up, we'll go get her. Just try to relax."

Relax? How could he do that when he didn't know if he'd ever see Billie again?

Up ahead on the road, Steven saw an overturned

truck, lit by headlights from other vehicles. People were running from the truck. From this far away, they looked as small and frantic as insects. Even at a distance, their fear was tangible.

He wondered if Billie was terrified right now. If she was, it was all his fault, he thought. If he'd bought a new car or kept his old one in better repair, then Billie never would have broken down and been delayed long enough to be caught alone when the earthquake hit. She'd warned him a hundred times that the rusty old Volkswagen was a death trap. He had always brushed aside her fears, claiming the Bug was a classic, and besides, he couldn't afford to have it overhauled. Now, because of his refusals, she was out there alone somewhere, maybe even hurt.

Steven had lost a girlfriend once before. Tricia Martin had been his first true love. She was a strawberry blonde with clear blue eyes and delicate features, and he'd sat helplessly by her bedside and watched her die a slow, painful death from leukemia. He had lost Tricia. He would not lose Billie.

Every fiber in Steven's body screamed out for him to find Billie, to be with her now, any way he could manage it. He peered at the road ahead, past the overturned truck and the scrambling insect-people. As close as he could figure it, the convenience store Billie had called from was at least four miles up the road. But the new Jeep was badly damaged.

Steven glanced at Jessica. She was just putting the first-aid kit away.

"Try the engine," he urged. "We can't just sit here." If the Wrangler couldn't make the trip, he would *run* all four miles. Nothing would stop him from reaching the woman he loved.

Ever since the earthquake, the Wakefields' backyard had been filled with a hideous symphony of sounds. Now Elizabeth heard a different kind of commotion, a noise that was actually cheerful. Her breath caught in her throat as she spun to look toward the house. Prince Albert was bounding toward her, barking an excited greeting. She ran to him and dropped to her knees, hugging him tightly while the dog licked her face.

The feathery softness of his fur brought back a flood of memories. When Jessica said she wanted to adopt a puppy without telling their parents, Elizabeth thought she was crazy. But Prince Albert was an adorable scamp with big paws and a totally lovable disposition. Elizabeth had taken one look and fallen in love. The twins had hidden Prince Albert in the basement.

Elizabeth remembered Jessica's frantic tears when the defenseless pup had disappeared. And she'd never forget the joy on her sister's face a few days later when Mr. Wakefield brought the twins a surprise—a puppy he'd found at the animal shelter. It was Prince Albert. Since that day he'd hardly spent a night anywhere but at the foot of Jessica's bed.

Now his golden coat was a filthy gray. Dust and grease rubbed off onto Elizabeth's blouse as she hugged him, but she didn't care. Suddenly she remembered that Prince Albert had been in the house when the earthquake began. She pulled away from the dog and looked him in the face as if expecting him to speak. Was anyone still trapped in the house?

She looked up in the direction he'd come from, and jumped to her feet when she saw three figures emerging from the smoke, coughing as they staggered across the yard together. Annie Whitman was in the middle, with Winston Egbert and Maria Santelli on either side of her, coaxing her along.

"Oh, Liz! Thank God you're all right," Maria

said, leaving Annie with Winston and rushing over to hug Elizabeth.

"Just a little bruised," Elizabeth said, embracing her friend. She was relieved to find someone else who seemed rational. "What's wrong with Annie?" Elizabeth asked.

"She's hurt, but it's not too bad," Maria answered.

Elizabeth looked at the others. "Winston!" she called, shocked at his pallor.

"I'm fine, Liz. I'll manage," he assured her. His eyes seemed a bit dazed, but his steps were sure and he was helping to support Annie.

Elizabeth hovered over them as Maria and Winston helped Annie to the ground. "Annie, where are you hurt?" Elizabeth asked.

"It's mainly just my arm," Annie said, shifting uncomfortably. "It's definitely broken."

Winston pulled his shirt off over his head and handed it to Maria. "Here. Maybe we can rip it up and make a sling out of it."

"Good thinking, Win," Maria said, starting a rip at the bottom hem.

Elizabeth suddenly felt awkward and in the way. Maria had this situation under control and Elizabeth was fairly useless. She hated being so scared, but it took every ounce of effort just to hold back the panic inside her.

She was grateful for Maria's presence. The daughter of Sweet Valley's mayor, Maria was a petite, dark-haired girl who seemed soft-spoken to people who didn't know her well. But she had a gift for organization and an iron will. Elizabeth was also a natural planner and leader. She usually worked well with Maria, but right now it was all she could do to stay calm and brave. She knew her facade was slipping.

Elizabeth took a deep breath and exhaled slowly. "Is anyone else still trapped inside?"

Annie nodded, her eyes glistening. "Ken and Olivia," she whispered.

"No!" Elizabeth's hand flew to her mouth, and she began to tremble. "Are they . . . they're not . . ." She couldn't bring herself to say it.

Maria and Winston exchanged a meaningful glance, and Elizabeth's stomach turned. Ken and Olivia were two of her best friends. They had to be OK.

"Ken is fine," Maria said slowly. "But Olivia . . ."

"Olivia's trapped, Liz," Winston broke in. "She's unconscious, and we're really not sure if she . . . if she made it."

Elizabeth's heart was in her throat. She

choked back a violent sob. "I have to go in there. I have to help them," she said frantically, the tears overflowing.

"You can't go in the house alone," Winston said, reaching out and touching her hand. "It's too dangerous."

Maria fiddled with the torn shirt in her hands. "There's nothing you can do anyway," she said. "Ken won't leave her side, but it's going to take more than two or three people to dig her out."

"Dig her out?" Elizabeth repeated slowly, quietly. She felt all of the energy draining out of her as the implications of that statement slowly sunk in. Her friends' faces were all tense, scared, and stricken. She couldn't imagine what it was they had seen, and she was certain she didn't want to know.

"We told Ken we'd be back with as many people as we could find, and we'd try to get the fire department as well," Winston said quickly.

"I can't just sit here and do nothing!" Elizabeth wailed. Olivia was one of her favorite people in the whole world. And her friends were telling her that Olivia might be . . . dead.

Winston reached over and wrapped his arm around Elizabeth while she sobbed. Maria slowly started to tie her makeshift sling around Annie's shoulder. As she lifted Annie's arm into the sling Annie winced but didn't cry out.

Elizabeth contained herself slowly. She didn't want to break down. Not now. She had to help her friends. She took a deep breath and stood up shakily, wiping her hands with her eyes. "Let me know if you guys are going to go back inside," Elizabeth said in a resigned voice, backing away from them. "I'll gather together anyone I find who's not hurt." *If they'll come,* she added silently. So far her efforts at organizing rescue teams had been dismal failures. But there were still so many people missing.

Suddenly Elizabeth spotted a figure lying in the grass, behind a hedge. It was too dark for her to see who the girl was. But everyone who'd come to her birthday party was important in some way to Elizabeth or her sister. "These people are my friends," she told herself as she squared her shoulders and walked toward the girl. "They need my help. I can't give up on them." *And I won't give up on Olivia,* she vowed silently.

Elizabeth rounded the hedge and found one of her best friends, Maria Slater. She took a sharp breath, dropped to her knees, and touched Maria's arm. It was warm. A good sign. Elizabeth had known Maria since elementary school, when the striking African American girl was a child actress and model. Maria had given up show business a few years back and moved to New York City. She had only recently returned to Sweet Valley and resumed her friendship with Elizabeth, but lately Elizabeth, Maria, and Enid had been practically inseparable.

Elizabeth put her hand under Maria's nose and felt her warm, ragged breathing.

"She's OK!" she called out to nobody in particular, sighing with relief. Only then did Elizabeth realize she'd been holding her own breath.

Maria had a nasty bump on the head, and Elizabeth realized that a piece of flying debris must have knocked her friend unconscious. Elizabeth hated seeing Maria lying motionless in the grass, but at least she felt as though she had a purpose now. Maria needed her. And helping her friend would occupy her mind, would keep her from speculating darkly about Jessica's whereabouts and Olivia's condition and . . . Todd. It was too dark behind the hedge to care for Maria's wounds, but she knew she shouldn't move an injured person—especially not someone with a head injury.

Elizabeth peered back toward the patio where

her friends were, hoping she could get one of them to bring her a candle so she could see if Maria was bleeding or cut anywhere. But she couldn't spot Winston, Maria, and Annie through the smoke, which was getting thicker. The orange glow in the sky had intensified. Behind the trees, beyond the Wakefields' yard, something was burning. She could hear the rustling of flames. It was coming from the Whitman-Thomas house next door, where Annie and her stepsister, Cheryl, lived with their newly married parents. *Annie must be frantic,* Elizabeth thought.

Suddenly she noticed another new sound, closer than the roar of the fire. Somewhere near the back of the yard something was sizzling and popping, with an odd, metallic buzz.

Elizabeth squinted through the haze, searching for the origin of the ominous noise. She froze. There, halfway underneath the back hedge, Enid Rollins lay, unmoving, in a puddle of water. Only a few feet from her head, exposed underground electrical wires squirmed like snakes, sending out showers of sparks.

"Enid!" Elizabeth screamed.

Maria was in no immediate danger. She'd be all right alone in the grass. But if one of those hot wires touched the water surrounding Enid, she could be electrocuted. Elizabeth sprang to her feet and sprinted toward her friend, praying she would reach Enid in time—if it wasn't already too late.

Lila pulled away from Todd and jumped to her feet. "What's that supposed to mean?" she demanded.

"What's what supposed to mean?" he asked, still sitting on the floor in the corner of the room.

"You said, 'Oh, no.'"

Todd rolled his eyes, infuriating her. "It means just what I said: 'Oh, no.' As in, 'We're in deep you-know-what.'"

"Don't be so melodramatic," Lila said. "So the light fixture busted. It wasn't that attractive anyhow."

"You're even more reality-impaired than I thought," Todd said with a sigh. "You have no idea how bad things are right now."

Lila gave him her most disdainful raised-eyebrow stare. "Believe me, I know exactly how bad things are," she said. "I'm stuck here with *you*, remember?"

"I'm not exactly thrilled with the company myself. But at the moment I'm more worried about the damage to this room."

Lila shrugged. "OK, one jar of expensive skin

cream is totally critical. But the rest of the stuff in the medicine cabinet wasn't important."

Todd sputtered.

"Someday, Todd, your brain may evolve to the point where you can form simple sentences."

"How's this for simple?" he asked acidly. *We have to get out of this house!*"

Lila rested her hands on her hips and glared down at him. "Well, duh. Or were you thinking we'd spend summer vacation in the Wakefields' bathroom?"

"Right. Like I'd spend my summer vacation with *you*," he retorted. "I'd rather eat ground glass."

She grabbed a paper cup from the dispenser and scooped up a handful of mirror chips that had fallen into the sink. She thrust the cup toward him. *"Bon appetit."*

"That's constructive."

"You are such a dweeb."

"Lila, we're trapped in this room," Todd said, rising to his feet. "And the house is going to crumble in on us. Soon."

She followed his gaze to a long horizontal crack along one wall. Above the crack, the wall was displaced a fraction of an inch to one side. She couldn't believe what a big deal he was making out of it. "Get a life, Wilkins. It's only a little crack."

"Lila, that little crack means structural damage. Horizontal cracks after an earthquake are bad news. And see how the wall's shifted? Another strong aftershock, and we're toast."

"You're a big, strong athlete," she told him. "Just break down the door, and we'll be out of here."

"I don't think that's possible," Todd said. "It's not just that the lock is jammed or something. The whole door frame's been crunched in."

"Todd, cops on television break down doors all the time. You just ram it with one of those testosterone-infused shoulders, and it busts open or smashes into kindling." She paused. "The door, not the shoulder," she added.

"Believe it or not," Todd began, "this isn't a TV show—"

"If it were, I'd fire the casting director," she replied. She pointed at the door. "At least try to act like a man."

Todd looked at her and then at the door. He took a deep breath and hurled himself across the room, slamming into the door with a loud thud and then sprawling on the floor. The hinges rattled, but the door remained stubbornly closed.

Lila didn't move to help as Todd brushed himself off and arranged his limbs, slowly, in a cross-legged position on the oval rug in the center of the room. He was breathing heavily and rubbing one shoulder. "As I said," he told her through clenched teeth, "the frame and the whole wall have shifted somehow. They're gripping that door like a vise."

"Can't you just break through the stupid thing?" Lila asked. "It doesn't look that thick."

"It's a metal door, Einstein."

Lila sat on the edge of the tub and pouted. "Some party this turned out to be. I should have known it would be a disaster."

"Like you could have predicted this?"

"Well, it *is* Friday the thirteenth," Lila reminded him. "We all should have just stayed home."

"I wish you had," Todd said evenly. He looked at his watch. "But it's not Friday the thirteenth for much longer," he said. "Midnight's only ten minutes away."

"Good," Lila said. "If I'm lucky, you'll turn into Prince Charming."

"And if *I'm* lucky, *you'll* turn into a frog."

"Why couldn't I be trapped here with someone interesting?" she demanded.

"I've got to hand it to you. You really know how to zero in on the most crucial aspects of a situation."

Lila stared at him until he looked away. The idea of being trapped in a small, dark room with a good-looking guy certainly had potential. And Todd was a hunk, with his six-foot-three frame, curly brown hair, and broad shoulders. Since his father had been made president of Varitronics, he even met Lila's second requirement for prospective boyfriends: He had money, though not nearly as much as her own family. But Jessica was right. He was the dullest guy in southern California—not to mention being the guy who had chosen Elizabeth Wakefield over both Lila and Jessica ages ago. There was no accounting for taste.

Lila assumed Todd was exaggerating about the structural damage to the house. What did he know, anyhow? It wasn't like he was some sort of architect or engineer. A lot of guys made up stuff just to scare girls, to build themselves up as big, fearless men. Well, Todd couldn't scare her. She hated the fact that he'd seen her display weakness earlier, and she vowed to keep her emotions in check from now on. Now that the aftershocks seemed to have slowed, she knew she wouldn't freak out again.

Being stuck with Todd, of all people, was by far the most dangerous thing about the evening, Lila told herself. If she didn't get away from him soon, he was in serious danger of becoming a murder victim.

"Make yourself useful," she said in her most imperious voice. "Find a way for us to get out of here."

"I don't take orders from you," he said.

Lila rose to her feet, crossed her arms, and stared down her nose at him. Some people were born to give orders, and others were born to follow them. She had no doubt about which group she belonged to. "It's your fault that we're stuck here," she told him. "Now you *will* find us a way out of this room."

"Or you'll do what?"

"Or I'll sue you for everything you're worth," she concluded triumphantly.

Todd narrowed his brown eyes at her. "For once in your life, why don't you just shut your trap?"

Lila gripped the edge of the sink with both hands. Nobody talked that way to her. She would make him sorry for treating her this way, if it was the last thing she did.

Chapter 5

Devon sat on the least damaged portion of the patio, his knees pulled to his chest. He'd never felt so lost and confused in his life. He still couldn't believe this was happening to him.

The whole world seemed to be on fire. Plumes of smoke rose in the distance like volcanoes in a prehistoric landscape. The air was thick with ash. The smell of acrid smoke overpowered everything else now, even the scent of chlorine from the swimming pool only a few feet away from him. Flames were shooting high into the air from the house and trees next door, lighting the entire sky.

A few intermittent flames had erupted from time to time in different parts of the Wakefield house, but so far they hadn't spread. But the blaze from next door was approaching, engulfing everything it touched. Soon what was left of the Wakefield house and yard would be crackling with flames.

He'd thought the earthquake was more frightening than anything else could ever be. But the fear he was experiencing now left him paralyzed. There was nowhere to run. The rubble from the house blocked one escape route to the street. And most of the trees on the other side of the yard, where people had gotten through earlier, were already starting to catch fire.

"Stay by the pool," he whispered to himself. If the fire got close, he could always jump in the water.

Suddenly he noticed a flash of blond hair on the far side of the yard. He thought it was Elizabeth, but he couldn't be sure through the smoke. Could it be Jessica? Devon couldn't remember if he'd seen Elizabeth's sister at all that night. Whoever it was, she was gingerly stepping alongside a tangle of exposed electrical lines that crackled and bristled with white-hot light, like Fourth of July sparklers. Surely it couldn't be Elizabeth, he told himself, his fists clenched in terror for her. She was too smart to fool around with something so dangerous. But the girl's blouse was a deep shade of pink, the same color Elizabeth had been wearing.

Devon rubbed his hands over his face, wondering if he should help her. He reminded himself that survival was his top priority. Getting himself electrocuted wouldn't do Elizabeth any good. Still, no matter how hard he tried to fight it, he knew in his heart that he was in love with Elizabeth. He had loved her since the first day he saw her.

Images of that day flooded his mind, and he laughed bitterly at the irony of it all. Devon had just moved to town, and he rode his motorcycle over to Sweet Valley High one day to check out his new school. There was a game that day, and Devon joined the crowd at the stadium.

Walking toward the bleachers, he was mesmerized by the sight of a beautiful blonde. Something about her was special. Sure, she was gorgeous, in a wholesome, girl-next-door kind of way. But it was more than her terrific figure and silky hair. She had an open, honest expression that caught his eye and touched his heart. Here, at last, was someone he thought he could trust. Someone he could love.

Of course, he knew now that he'd been dead wrong about the trust part. Elizabeth had pretended to choose Devon over Todd Wilkins. In the end, she couldn't make up her mind, and she'd betrayed them both.

But the day he first glimpsed her at the crowded stadium, he couldn't have known that would happen. All he knew was that he had to make her love him. He'd watched Elizabeth until she disappeared into the throng. Minutes later an explosion ripped through the school, and Sweet Valley High erupted in flames.

Devon remembered hearing screams and cries, watching people scramble around in all directions. A few had suffered minor injuries. And John Pfeifer, the student who'd set the bomb, was dead. The explosion blew apart the school gym and terrified a lot of people. But Devon's life hadn't been in danger that day. Those in the stadium were never at risk. Besides, help had arrived within minutes. He remembered the flash of colored lights from the police cars, the efficiency of the ambulance attendants, and the trill of sirens from the fire engines.

The situation in the Wakefield yard was completely different. The smell of smoke was the same, but here it would only keep getting thicker. The fire would come closer, would envelop the whole yard. It was only a matter of time. Devon knew he couldn't count on help from the authorities. The whole town, maybe the whole coast, had been devastated. It might be hours before a rescue squad could get around to one little backyard on Calico Drive.

"Devon!" a girl's voice called. "Devon, is that you?" Maria Santelli and Winston Egbert were running toward him.

Winston put a hand on Devon's shoulder, and Devon shrugged it away. Winston seemed too dazed to notice.

"Whitelaw, do you have a cell phone?" Winston asked.

Devon tensed. Just because he'd inherited some money, everyone assumed he was into every expensive hobby and owned every high-tech gadget. "What does that have to do with anything?"

"Some people are trapped in the house," Maria explained, speaking quickly. "We need to call nine-one-one."

"I don't have a phone," Devon said, shielding his eyes from the bright glow of flames as he looked up at her. "But what's the point? Do you really think the fire department is going to drop everything and rush over here?"

"Yes, I do," Maria cried.

71

Devon swept a hand toward the house. "Reality check time," he announced. "In case you haven't noticed, we're in the middle of a major natural disaster."

"No kidding," Winston said. "And we thought it was the world's biggest weenie roast."

"And you're the world's biggest weenie. Dammit, Egbert, that last aftershock took down half the roof. Nobody is alive in there!"

"Don't say that," Maria said.

"Those are our friends in there," Winston said tersely. "We have to try!"

"Well, there's nothing I can do for you," Devon replied.

"Have you seen Bruce Patman?" Maria asked. "I know he's got a phone. But no one knows where he is."

Devon nodded and half smirked. "Yeah, I saw him. He had the sense to blow this joint while there was still a chance of getting away without being charbroiled."

"He's gone?" Maria asked. "Are you sure?"

"I saw him run out just after the first quake. Mumbled something about getting home to the family mansion. I bet he pays the servants there to shield him with their bodies."

"What about Lila?" Winston asked. "Nobody's seen her either."

Devon shrugged. "Fowler probably has cell phones in every color, to match her outfits. But I don't have a clue about where to find her."

Winston and Maria looked at each other. "She's been missing since the first earthquake," Maria said. "I hope she's not lying somewhere hurt." She gulped visibly. "Or worse."

"Her car was in the driveway," Winston said, his voice suddenly hopeful. "I bet she's got a phone in there. If I can make my way around the side of the house—"

"Don't you morons get it?" Devon interrupted, surprised to hear himself shouting. "You can't get there from here! Nobody is alive in that house. And in another hour, hardly anyone in this yard will be alive either." *Except me,* he vowed silently.

"Devon, you're panicking," Maria said softly, her lips set in a thin, tight line. She began to cough, and Winston patted her on the back until she could continue speaking. "We have to stay calm. We can all get out of this alive if we work together."

Devon rolled his eyes. "Next you'll want us to link arms and sing, 'The sun will come out tomorrow.'"

Maria's eyes flashed. She opened her mouth as

if to protest, but she closed it abruptly and clenched her fists at her sides. A few seconds later she spoke, her voice low and steady. "While Winston tries to get to Lila's phone, you can help me organize a rescue team, Devon. We have to dig our way back into the house. That aftershock blocked the route Winston used before."

Devon shook his head. "The only way any of us is going to make it through the next few hours is by playing it safe. No unnecessary risks."

"The risk is totally necessary," Winston said. "Ken and Olivia are trapped in there. Maybe some others too. Including Todd."

Devon hooted. "Wilkins? You want me to risk my life for the guy Liz cheated on me with?"

"Is that all you can think about at a time like this?" Maria asked. "Your wounded male pride?"

Winston grabbed her arm. Devon watched as an expression of total disgust contorted Winston's features. He didn't care. "Come on, Maria," Winston said. "No sense wasting time on this loser. We've got work to do."

Olivia was freezing. Why was she so cold? And what was happening to her? Had she been asleep? Olivia opened her eyes, but the air around her was as dark as the inside of her eyelids and seemed haunted by terrifying images of orange flames, of walls shredded to kindling, and of something dark and enormous hurtling toward her from overhead. Earsplitting noises tore through the air. Pain squeezed every part of her body—crushing, bruising, stabbing pains like nothing she'd ever imagined, let alone experienced.

It's a nightmare, she told herself. Any minute now her mother would glide into her room and shake her awake, looking ordinary and comforting in one of the sensible suits Olivia had always thought boring. She'd tell her to get up for another ordinary, comforting day of school.

Suddenly Olivia smelled smoke and remembered. This wasn't her messy, disorganized bedroom. It was chaos in its most terrifying form. She was buried in the rubble of the Wakefields' kitchen, after an earthquake more powerful than anything she'd ever felt. She knew she was hurt badly, maybe critically. She could hardly move at all. Her head was spinning, making it hard to focus.

The coldness is shock, she told herself slowly. She tried to remember what Ms. Rice had said in the first-aid unit of her health class. People in shock should be kept warm. But there were no blankets here.

Gradually Olivia became aware of a presence nearby. A comforting warmth enveloped her right hand. She squinted, trying hard to see straight. "Ken?" she whispered.

"Hey, Livvy," he said, his voice as soothing as his touch on her hand.

She took a deep breath, and she winced as a pain sliced through her chest like a knife. She coughed, and his hand tightened on hers. "How bad do I look?" she asked finally.

Ken smiled. He was dirty and disheveled. His clothes were torn and his blond hair was grayed with dust. But his smile was heartbreakingly handsome, and Olivia knew she'd never seen anything so wonderful.

"You look beautiful," he responded gently.

Olivia smiled back at him weakly. "That's not what I meant," she whispered. "How bad do my injuries look? Am I gonna be OK?"

She saw the flash of fear in his eyes, but Ken recovered in a second. When he smiled again, his jaw was tense. "Don't worry about a thing," he assured her. "You're going to be fine."

Olivia wished she could believe him, but a strange numbness was beginning to creep through her body, like the moon's shadow stealing across the sun, slowly but inexorably. As the numbness crept over her, tingling at first, the pain began to subside.

Ken leaned over and kissed her on the forehead, his lips soft and warm against her cold skin. "We'll get you out of here," he promised. "Winston and Maria ran for help."

So Maria was OK. Olivia thought back to before the earthquake. It seemed like weeks ago. A wave of dizziness blanketed her, and she squeezed her eyes shut until it passed. Somebody else had been in the kitchen, she remembered. She had to know if her friends were all right.

"Annie?" she asked in a frightened whisper.

"She broke her arm and has a bump on her head," Ken said. "But she was able to walk out of here with only a little help."

Olivia tried to nod, relieved, but her head felt as heavy as the smooth, rectangular mass that pinned her down. It was the Wakefields' refrigerator, she realized groggily. She suddenly remembered the earthquake's first rumblings. She'd stood with her back against this same appliance, grateful for the solid, cool comfort of it through the thin cotton of her dress. Its size and stability had reassured her then. Now Olivia knew they were an illusion. The earthquake was more powerful. It could toss a refrigerator across the room like a child's plastic block or hurl the ceiling onto the floor. In seconds its awesome force could turn beauty and light into devastation and despair.

Tears prickled the edges of her eyelids, and Olivia blinked rapidly. Ken stroked her cheek with his warm, gentle hands. She gazed into his eyes, and the desolation receded.

Again Ken was speaking of her impending rescue, promising to stay by her side until help arrived. His voice sounded fuzzy and far away. He wanted to comfort her, she knew, and to convince himself that she would be all right. He couldn't bear to face the truth. She didn't blame him. But Olivia refused to lie to herself. She knew what the creeping numbness could mean—paralysis, or even death. The numbness terrified her, but she welcomed it too. It would mean freedom from the crushing pain that still racked most of her body.

Olivia squeezed Ken's hand. Then she closed her eyes and slipped back into the moon's shadow.

"Come on, baby. Come on," Jessica urged. She turned the key in the Jeep's ignition. It revved with a low whine, but the engine wouldn't turn over.

"Start the car, already!" Steven yelled.

Jessica whirled on him. The moon had slipped

behind a cloud, and his face was in shadow, but his voice was totally impatient. "Start the car? What a brilliant plan. Why didn't I think of that? In case you haven't noticed, we've got a telephone pole for a hood ornament."

"I can do without the sarcasm."

"And I can do without you treating me like an idiot!"

"Sorry," Steven said with a sigh. "But please try the engine again. We have to get this thing started, Jess. She's all by herself!"

"Check under the hood—if it'll open," Jessica suggested. *Poor Elizabeth,* she thought. At least Jessica had her brother with her. And their parents had each other. Elizabeth didn't have a single family member around to comfort her, unless you counted Prince Albert.

Steven jumped out of the Jeep and managed to wrench the hood open after Jessica pulled the release.

"Can you fix it?" she asked immediately. "Can you tell what's wrong? Do you know why it won't start?"

He put his hands on his hips. "I imagine it has something to do with the fact that the vehicle is wrapped around a telephone pole."

"Now who's being sarcastic?"

"I'm a prelaw student, not an auto mechanic," Steven said. "I wish Liz were here. She knows more about fixing cars than either of us."

At the mention of her sister's name, Jessica was stunned by a rush of dizzy terror. She gripped the steering wheel, and her knuckles shone as white as bare bones. She'd been trying to explain away the panic and fear that kept flashing through her head. She'd told herself it was her own anxieties that had her so much on edge. But now she had to admit the truth: The twin sense was setting off red-alert buzzers in her brain.

Steven fiddled with something under the hood. "Try the engine now," he urged.

Jessica turned the key again, but the engine refused to start. She blinked back tears of fear and frustration. Elizabeth was scared, maybe in terrible danger, and Jessica couldn't even coax the Jeep into starting.

"We have to get to her!" Jessica whispered, pounding her fists on the steering wheel in desperation. She had to make it home, whatever it took. Her twin needed her.

Again she twisted the key in the ignition, saying a silent little prayer. But this time the engine sputtered to life. Jessica let out a shout of joy.

"Yes!" Steven cheered, giving her a thumbs-up. The hood clanged discordantly when he slammed it shut. Jessica crossed her fingers, desperately hoping the Jeep was healthy enough to traverse the distance to Calico Drive. Steven climbed into the passenger seat and Jessica threw the car into reverse. She pulled back onto the road, worried by an ominous rattle from the engine but relieved to be in motion at last.

As soon as Jessica started trying to maneuver, she realized that getting home would be more difficult than she'd anticipated. Parts of the windshield had been smashed in by the force of the crash. It was laced by a network of cracks that obscured her view, and Jessica found herself dodging and shifting as she drove, trying to catch a clear glimpse of the road ahead.

The street was damaged as well. The pavement was buckled and twisted into a landscape of craters and rocky lumps. Negotiating its hills and valleys was like driving through an obstacle course. Usually Jessica's preferred driving speed was fast, if not faster. Now she knew that one mistake at the wheel could completely disable the already sputtering Jeep. Her head was buzzing with Elizabeth's fear, as if her twin were sending out distress calls. But she couldn't help Elizabeth if the Jeep broke down miles from home. Jessica choked back her panic and concentrated on the road, trying not to look at the caved-in houses and burning businesses they were passing.

"So much destruction," Steven said slowly, in a desolate whisper that sent chills down Jessica's spine. "I hope she's OK."

Jessica glanced at his stark face and swallowed a sob. She knew her twin wasn't OK. Elizabeth's fear and desperation were as palpable in Jessica's mind as Jessica's own terror.

She forced herself to fix an image in her thoughts, an image of Elizabeth, safe and smiling. In Jessica's mental picture, her sister was fiddling with the gold lavaliere she always wore around her neck, the necklace that was the identical twin of the one Jessica wore. The lavalieres had been gifts from the twins' parents on the girls' sixteenth birthday, exactly one year ago. Jessica grasped her own necklace now and held it tightly, wishing she could send her sister a message of peace and safety.

A few minutes later she breathed a deep sigh, seeing a familiar intersection up ahead. A bent street sign lay across the lane in front of her, and she veered around it. Downtown Sweet Valley, the sign said, with an arrow that was usually pointing left. The way to Calico Drive led to the right.

Suddenly Steven yelled. A deep black crack had opened up in the roadway, a thick, jagged streak that tore through the concrete like a lightning bolt. The crevasse was wide enough to trap a tire. Jessica wrenched the steering wheel to the left and swerved sharply around it.

At that moment the Jeep bucked and shivered. Something roared hugely in Jessica's ears, drowning out other sounds and even her thoughts. A powerful vibration threatened to tear her apart. For an instant she was sure the entire Jeep was falling, impossibly, into the dark, narrow crack. Jessica screamed. Her eyes widened in horror as a cypress tree by the side of the road wrenched itself from the earth's grasp. Its roots hung, quivering, in the air for what seemed like an eternity. Then the tree crashed to the road's shoulder, one misshapen branch scraping against Jessica's window as it fell. The roar subsided.

Jessica braked, right there in the intersection, and closed her eyes, resting her forehead on the steering wheel as she tried to control her breath. Her hands were trembling. "An aftershock," Steven said, panting. When she forced her eyes open, she saw her brother leaning back in his seat, his face as pale as the moon. He opened his eyes and they stared at each other for a few seconds. Jessica nodded and took a deep breath. They were still alive. They had to go on.

She revved the engine back to life and they circled the center of the intersection to make the right turn toward Calico Drive.

Suddenly Steven reached for the wheel. "Where do you think you're going?" he demanded.

Jessica blinked, wondering if the earthquake had shaken something loose in her brother's head. She shoved his hand out of the way. "Where do *you* think I'm going? Home, of course."

"Home?" he bellowed, his eyes wide.

"Yes, home," Jessica repeated, continuing to drive. "Where else would I be going?"

"You can't!" Steven cried, his eyes wild. He grabbed at the wheel again, and the car swerved with a piercing screech of tires.

"Steven!" Jessica screamed.

Chapter 6

Elizabeth skirted the swimming pool as she made her way across the glistening patio toward Enid. Suddenly something slammed into Elizabeth from below, as if a giant, burrowing animal were butting against the soles of her shoes. The flagstone patio beneath her was rocking. She slipped on a stone that had been thrust upward and stumbled to her knees. Her body was hurtling forward, toward the surface of the swimming pool. She clutched wildly at an overturned patio table to break her fall. Then she crouched there, hanging on to the table to ride out the aftershock.

A roar erupted from what was left of her family's house. She watched, gasping for air, as another section of the roof collapsed like a burst balloon.

Ken and Olivia were in the house, and it was possible that Todd was too. Elizabeth squeezed her eyes shut, unable to distinguish the earth's shaking from the trembling of her own body. *Why is this happening to us?* she wondered.

As the aftershock subsided, Elizabeth picked herself up slowly and tried to figure out the safest way to reach Enid. Her best friend lay, faceup and unconscious, in a shallow pool of water. Elizabeth wondered how the water had reached that far back in the yard, but a rushing sound answered her question. The pool pump pipes had surfaced through the patio and were spouting water everywhere.

Enid's fair complexion was drained of color. Her reddish brown hair fanned out around a pleasant, round face that suddenly looked much younger than her sixteen years. Terror gripped Elizabeth as she focused on the fallen electrical lines that squirmed near her friend like electric eels. Fountains of sparks cascaded from their ends, and they emitted a buzzing sound that reminded Elizabeth of bug zappers.

She looked up sharply, hearing a new note of panic in the cries around her. The aftershock must have further damaged the Whitman-Thomas house, she realized with a sinking heart. Billows of smoke were rising faster from behind the trees. The crackle of flames sounded louder.

Elizabeth knew that what she was about to do was terribly dangerous. She would have to edge along the length of the exposed wires, only inches from where they writhed, before she could reach Enid and drag her to safety. The ground was wet, and it was dotted with puddles, some more than ankle-deep. Electricity could travel through water. If one of those dancing wires grazed her, or even touched a puddle she was wading through, she could be electrocuted on the spot.

"Somebody help me!" Elizabeth wailed. "Can anyone hear me?" She looked around, but the smoke was so thick she could barely keep her eyes open. Where were Winston and Maria? Where were Amy, Barry, and A.J.? And Devon? Had they all climbed over the rubble and deserted her? Had Devon left her back here to perish?

Elizabeth didn't think she could handle this alone. "But if I don't try, Enid could die," she said aloud, rubbing at the tears she suddenly found on her own face. Elizabeth would not abandon her friend. She threw back her shoulders and straightened her chin. "Be calm," she told herself.

She had to move slowly and carefully. One

misstep could mean the end for both herself and Enid. She took a small, deliberate step toward her friend.

A loud bark startled her and she almost tripped. Elizabeth turned to see the dog standing a few feet away, wagging his feathery tail in a show of support. "No, Prince Albert!" she begged. "Don't you dare follow me!"

It was bad enough that her whole family might be in terrible danger, or worse. She wasn't about to lose Prince Albert too. She stared a warning at him until he raised his head and sniffed cautiously in the direction of the sparks. He barked once, then ambled away. Then Elizabeth inched forward, her eyes on the undulating electrical wires near her feet. Their glowing ends slashed ghostly, white-hot patterns in the darkness.

Suddenly a terrible scream rang out through the backyard. Elizabeth, caught off guard, narrowly missed stepping on a wire. She jumped out of the way.

She couldn't tell who had screamed, but she immediately knew why. The fire next door was spreading toward her own backyard. The row of trees was on fire, blazing like giant torches. Closer, tongues of flame already lapped at the Wakefields' wooden fence. With bitter clarity, Elizabeth knew exactly what would happen next. The blaze would leap from tree to tree. It would work its way to the rubble of Elizabeth's house, and the pile of debris would become a bonfire. Everyone in the yard was in terrible danger. The wounded, especially, could be trapped in the path of the flames. Soon what was left of her own house and yard would be an inferno.

Elizabeth's courage evaporated into the smoke-filled night. She began to tremble again. There was no use trying to save Enid or anyone else who was hurt. She might be able to pull her best friend away from the electrical wires, but she'd never be able to carry her out of the fire's path.

A stray reflection of light caught the face of Elizabeth's watch, and she started. It was midnight. The twins' seventeenth birthday was over.

Olivia had always wondered what it would be like to die. She'd never expected to feel such . . . calm. And so much love for the guy kneeling beside her in the middle of such destruction. A strong aftershock had precipitated a terrifying series of crashes. She was sure that another part of the house had caved in, but she couldn't see the new damage. From Ken's grim expression, she knew that Winston's promised rescue would be delayed.

The air felt heavy and gritty in her lungs. But the numbness had claimed half her body. She could no longer move much of anything, except for her head.

"Ken," she whispered, nearly choking with the effort to speak. "Touch me. I want to feel you close by." She knew he was holding her hand, could see his fingers around hers. But she couldn't feel them.

"I'm here, Olivia," he said, reaching out to stroke her face.

She remembered the exact moment she'd fallen in love with Ken. She'd been chatting on-line with the boy she still knew only as Quarter. And he'd invited her to a private chat room, so he could give her a virtual gift. She'd been thrilled to read on her monitor that he'd picked her a flower. He described it to her, the words appearing on her screen seconds after he keyed them in on his own computer.

"It's a bright, passionate red," he typed, *"the reddest red you can ever imagine. Vivid, like the pictures you paint with words."*

Olivia had never heard anything so romantic. She'd urged him to tell her more.

"Its petals are as thin as tissue paper, fragile. But they're soft and warm. And inside, there are these black thready things. The red and black together are awesome."

Ken wasn't a practiced poet, like Olivia. But he had a clear, straightforward way of expressing himself that had completely blown her away. She'd never met a boy who was so warm and thoughtful. The guys she'd dated in the real, nonvirtual world certainly wouldn't think to pick a wildflower for her. And they'd never have the confidence to describe it on-line in such detail. They'd be too afraid of sounding sappy.

Now she looked into his dark-lashed blue eyes and marveled at her luck in finding somebody so good for her. If she was really going to die that night, her biggest regret was losing out on a future spent with Ken.

The numbness was spreading, but with it came peace. As Ken touched her face with strong, tender hands, she turned her head to kiss his fingers. "Remember the poppy?" she whispered.

He smiled, but his eyes were sad. "Always."

Olivia smiled back, but her head was feeling fuzzy again. She opened her mouth to tell him something but began to cough instead. Ken's jaw clenched, and she felt terrible about scaring him so badly.

"Don't try to talk now," he said softly. "Save your strength."

He was probably right. And she knew she couldn't keep up a conversation much longer, even if she wanted to. But there was one thing she had to tell him. "I love you, Quarter."

"I love you too, Freeverse," he replied. "More than anything in the world."

She was happy to hear the words, but she'd already known how he felt. She could feel his love washing over her like a soft, balmy rain shower on a summer day. If she had to die, she was grateful that the last voice she'd ever hear would be Ken's, and that the last sensation she'd ever feel would be the warmth of his love.

Steven wanted to scream with frustration when Jessica pulled the Jeep off the crumpled road surface. They would never reach Billie at this rate. But trying to negotiate the cracked and buckled roadway while screaming at each other just wasn't safe.

"Are you insane, yanking the steering wheel away from me like that?" Jessica demanded as soon as the Jeep was still. "You could've gotten us both killed!"

"You were going the wrong way," Steven accused.

"And you're going postal! Why do you think we were so frantic about getting the Jeep started? So we could get home! And home is this way." She pointed.

Steven shook his head. "Jess, I know you're worried about Liz, but—"

"Worried? I've got a thousand horror movies playing in my head at double speed. Elizabeth is in trouble. We have to get to her."

"But—"

"What could be more important than rescuing our sister? Let me guess. You suddenly remembered you have to pick up paper clips at the school-supply store."

"Of course I'm concerned about Liz. And about the kids at the party. And about Mom and Dad, for that matter." He grabbed her arm. "But none of them is stranded and alone. Billie is!"

"We have no reason to think Billie's hurt," Jessica reminded him. "And we *know* Elizabeth is terrified. I can feel her."

"Billie's only about four miles from here, and it's all straight, easy roads," he said, trying to sound cool and logical. "Home is twice as far away in the other direction, and the roads twist a lot. It'll take us longer to get there."

"Then that's all the more reason to start now!" Jessica cried, her eyes filling with tears. Steven took a deep breath and tried to sound soothing, even though he was in super freak-out mode himself.

"Billie is stranded," Steven reminded her. "The car's broken down. If we don't pick her up, she's stuck there, all by herself. At least Liz is at home, surrounded by friends."

"They're my friends too!" Jessica said. The tears shone in her blue-green eyes, and she looked down at her hands. "But it's Elizabeth I'm worried about. I feel like I'm being ripped apart not knowing if she's OK. I *know* she's in danger."

Despite Jessica's special connection with her twin, Steven had to believe that Elizabeth was unhurt. It was the only way he could convince himself to put Billie first. "You don't know that for sure," he said.

Jessica whirled on him. "Yes, I do! And if *she's* in danger at home, then everyone else might be too. Lila's there, and Annie, and Maria . . . Except for you and Mom and Dad, almost every person I care about is at our house right now. They might even be dying. I have to get to them!"

Steven was afraid she would burst out in sobs,

but he knew he had to keep pushing. Billie's life might depend on it. "That's exactly what I mean," he said. "Outside of our family, every person *I* care about is stranded in a broken-down Volkswagen!"

"But Steven—"

"Think about it. Dozens of people are at the party with Liz. And Mom and Dad are together. If one of them is injured, we know someone will be nearby to help. They don't need us as badly as Billie does!" He stared into her eyes, pleading.

Jessica was crying softly. "I like Billie," she said, her voice rough with tears. "You know I do. And I'm scared for her. But Steven, this is Elizabeth we're talking about!"

Steven felt tears on his own cheeks now. He grabbed his sister's hands and squeezed them. "Jessica, the thought of Billie out there alone in this war zone is tearing me up inside. I promise you, we'll race to her as quickly as we can, and then get right back to Calico Drive to help Elizabeth and the others."

Jessica stared at Steven, her eyes wide. "What if it's too late by then?"

Olivia's head fell back limply. Every time she

drifted into unconsciousness, Ken felt paralyzed by fear. He moved his fingers on her throat until he felt a faint, thready pulse. His own pulse was pounding hard enough for them both.

He slumped back and closed his eyes. Olivia was still alive, but he didn't know for how much longer. He couldn't even reach all of her body to assess her injuries. She was still partially pinned down by the heavy refrigerator and the second ceiling beam.

One of her legs was crushed, a splinter of bone gleaming white through the dark flow of blood. A gash on her head, combined with her dizziness and dilated eyes, probably meant a concussion. Her body was twisted beneath the debris, and she couldn't feel her legs anymore, so he had to assume she had a spinal injury as well. Her left arm and shoulder were beneath the refrigerator, but she'd told him earlier that she was sure the arm was broken. Now she had no sensation in it. And bright bursts of blood stained the front of her print dress like a sick parody of the tie-dye fashions she loved to wear.

Scariest of all was the possibility of internal injuries he could only begin to guess at. In the last few minutes before she fainted, she'd begun coughing up blood.

Her face was peaceful now—and lovely, despite the deep cut on her forehead. He stood slowly and circled the refrigerator again, trying to puzzle out any way of freeing her. He'd already tried all the obvious ways to move the heavy appliance. He'd even attempted to lift it with a lever made from a stick of wood he'd broken off a chair. But every time he so much as nudged the refrigerator, Olivia screamed out in agony. She'd lost feeling in her arms and legs, but she still felt pain, terrible pain, in her head and midsection. Every cry from her mouth burned like a sword thrust into his heart.

Suddenly Ken froze. Muffled voices were speaking somewhere in the rubble. A guy and a girl. He couldn't hear the words, but it had to be Maria and Winston, returning to help him.

"Egbert?" he called. The only answer was a loud thud as a chunk of drywall slid to the floor. He sighed. The voices were all in his mind. They had to be. As far as he could tell, the latest aftershock had imploded what had been left of the house's second story, sending more debris cascading to the first floor. The narrow path where he'd watched Winston's back dissolve into the smoke was blocked now. His friends—and any professionals they managed to summon—would have to dig a new way in. And that could take hours.

"Are you still there?" called a thin, frightened voice. Olivia coughed weakly.

He sprang to her side, mortified that she'd woken up to find herself alone. "Don't be scared," he told her. "I'm here." Her pulse was even weaker than before. He stroked her wild brown curls. They were streaked with grease and dust, but they still felt like Olivia.

She was always complaining about her hair. She considered it too unusual, too frizzy and unruly. But Ken always said it suited her creative spirit. Besides, he thought it was sexy.

Olivia closed her eyes as if the long-lashed lids were too heavy to hold open. "Talk to me," she whispered. "Talk about the good times we had."

Ken's heart turned. She'd said *had*, past tense, as if she was sure there'd be no more good times for her.

Touching her hair reminded him of a trip they'd taken together in the early days of their relationship. It had been a cybertrip, actually. She was still Freeverse and he was still Quarter, and they had never met in person. Their virtual trips had been special to them both. Connected by nothing more than modems and phone lines, they would envision a scene together, taking turns describing what it looked like and what they would say and do, as if it were really happening.

"Remember our virtual ski trip?" he asked her. "It was our first kiss, and we weren't even in the same room."

Olivia smiled, her eyes still closed. "Tell me," she urged.

Olivia floated in a haze of smoke and dizziness, tethered only by Ken's warm, husky voice. She was a child again, and her parents were telling her a bedtime story, about a place that was happy and full of love.

No, she reminded herself. She had to stop letting her mind drift off like that. It was Ken who was telling her a story. It was a true story, and she was the main character.

The cybertrip was a ski vacation at Snow Mountain. Olivia had spent spring break that year at the Colorado resort, on a school trip with some of their classmates. Ken had missed the trip, but online together, Freeverse and Quarter imagined the interior of a cozy log cabin near the slopes.

As a fire crackled merrily on the stone hearth of

their cyberretreat, snow fell outside the windows and frost etched the glass. Outside, a full moon bathed the woods in a soft, milky light.

Olivia mentioned the cold weather, and Ken—as Quarter—offered to warm her by slipping his arm around her shoulders. Neither had seen the other in person, so they stopped to describe themselves.

"When I say 'curly,' I really mean curly," she'd told him, typing the words and then sending them through cyberspace to his machine. *"It's thick and wild and long and frizzy. The kind of hair people refer to as a 'curly mop' or a 'wild mane.'"*

"Awesome!" Quarter replied, the word on her screen surprising her with its enthusiasm. *"Most of the girls I know all have the same two or three hairstyles."* His comments lit a warm glow deep inside her. A lot of the guys at school thought she was just plain weird. Quarter made her feel that being different was special.

"I think I would like to run my fingers through those wild, sexy curls," he said.

"Only if I can touch your hair too," she typed back, mesmerized by his words and shocked at her own courage.

"Your hair is gorgeous, Free," wrote Quarter. *"It feels like silk, and all those curls are shimmering*

in the firelight. And now my hand strokes the side of your face, and your skin is as soft as the petal of a poppy."

As Ken recounted this part of their online conversation, he again stroked the side of her face. "I can feel your fingertips," she whispered, remembering that those were the exact words she'd typed in response.

A few minutes later in their cybercabin, Olivia had warned Quarter that she wasn't pretty. He had stopped her. He invented a new rule: only objective detail was allowed, no negative judgments. *"Paint a picture in my mind,"* he'd urged her, *"like you're collecting images for a poem."* So she'd described herself as clearly as she could. Then Quarter surprised her with his next question: *"What do you like about yourself?"*

The question was a revelation to Olivia. When she thought of her looks, it was always in terms of what she *didn't* like. Her hair was too crazy. Her face was too round. She longed for the perfect, regular features of fashion models, to be conventionally beautiful, like the Wakefield twins or Lila Fowler. But Ken had forced her to look at herself in a new light.

"My hands," she'd decided suddenly, typing the words. *"I like my hands!"*

101

He'd described taking her hands in his and stroking her fingers with his. Then he was kissing her via modem, more sensually than any real kiss she'd experienced at the time.

"And then you kiss me back, Freeverse, long and hard," he'd typed. *"And nothing has ever rocked me the way your kiss does."*

Olivia had stared breathlessly at his words on her computer monitor. *"And we hold each other tightly as the flames cast orange-and-red tongues of light around the room,"* she added.

"And your body feels soft and warm," Ken had concluded, *"and fits perfectly against mine."*

The memories were warm, but she realized she was shivering. Ken leaned over, rubbing her arm with his hand. "Stay with me, Livvy," he urged. "You've got to hang in there until Winston and Maria can make it back with a rescue team."

Olivia shook her head almost imperceptibly. "Ken—"

"No!" he cried, one hand cradling the side of her face. "We can't give up hope."

Olivia smiled and kissed the palm of his hand. "Have I mentioned how much I love you?" she asked him, the words rasping in her throat like sandpaper.

"Not half as much as I love you," he replied. "I won't leave you, Livvy, no matter what happens."

Olivia gazed up into Ken's eyes, so full of pain and grief. In them, she saw the realization he couldn't bring himself to admit. He might not want to leave her. But if help didn't arrive soon, she might have to leave him. Forever.

Chapter 7

"I can't believe you're still arguing about this! We're wasting time and we're not helping anyone just sitting here," Steven yelled. "Think about Billie!"

Jessica could hear the frustration in his voice, but she couldn't believe what he was saying. Abandon their sister? "Think about Elizabeth!"

"You're being immature and selfish," Steven accused, staring her down.

"Are you insane?" Jessica flared with anger. "I'm not thinking about myself. I'm worried about Liz!"

Jessica covered her face with her hands, trying to rein in her emotions. As much as she hated being called immature, she had to admit that her protests were beginning to sound lame, even to herself. From an objective point of view, there was no reason to think her twin was in any graver danger than anyone else in town. Sure, the twin sense told her Elizabeth was terrified. But if she could sense Billie's state of mind, she'd no doubt feel fear from Steven's girlfriend too. Anyone in Sweet Valley who wasn't scared stiff on this night was either stupid, comatose, or totally wiggy.

Steven lowered his voice. "I think you're getting too wrapped up in your panic—or Elizabeth's panic, if that's really what you're feeling. You're letting it cloud your judgment."

Jessica leaned forward and rested her forehead on the steering wheel. Her hair fell over her face like a curtain, hiding her from Steven while she tried to sort out her emotions and thoughts. By choosing to go after Billie first, she felt as though she were ripping her own heart out. It wasn't fair that she had to make such terrible decisions.

Finally she looked at her brother and nodded slowly. "You're right," she admitted. "I'm so freaked for Liz that I can hardly think straight." Steven had a point. Two points, actually. Elizabeth was among friends, while Billie was alone. And they were closer to Billie's location. They could reach her sooner. She swallowed hard. "We'll go for Billie first."

Steven hugged her quickly, then yanked a handkerchief from the pocket of his jeans and carefully wiped the tears from her face. Jessica pulled back onto the road and headed toward downtown Sweet Valley—away from Calico Drive. Behind her she felt the force of her sister's panic, as tangible as the upended trees that littered the road. It was like the feeling of being alone in a dark, lonely place, with the creepy sensation that a pair of eyes was watching her from behind. No matter how far she drove, she knew, she couldn't escape the eyes. Not until she saw for herself that Elizabeth was safe.

She squeezed the gold lavaliere between her fingers, wishing it could transport her to her sister's side, like Dorothy's ruby slippers.

"It looks like we're not in Kansas anymore," she whispered grimly, shuddering as she drove past a house that had collapsed so thoroughly that its upstairs windows were now where the door should be. She couldn't bear to think of what her own house might look like right now. And here she was, driving in the opposite direction. In all of Jessica's seventeen years, she had never felt more powerless.

❈   ❈   ❈

107

Elizabeth had never felt more powerless. For the moment, the smoke from the fire raging next door was blowing in a different direction. And the flames themselves were near enough to illuminate more of the Wakefield yard in their flickering, red-gold glow. What Elizabeth could see by their light was horrifying.

Elizabeth's friends hadn't all deserted her, but from the looks of things, they were trying desperately to get out of the yard. Normally they would be able to walk around either side of the house, but the structure had shifted to the side and dumped rubble over one exit. The other side was blocked by raging fire. A bunch of people were scrambling to dig through the debris and open up a pathway.

Another group of figures clustered near the back of the house, close to the spot where the sliding glass doors to the kitchen had been. Someone had found a flashlight, and it cast bizarre shadows behind the group, wraithlike shadows that lengthened and shrank and flickered like flame. One of the figures turned, and Elizabeth recognized Maria Santelli. The people seemed to be digging. Elizabeth held her breath. Maybe they were trying to venture back into the rubble after Ken and Olivia. Maybe they would even find Todd.

A single tear rolled down Elizabeth's face. "Who am I kidding?" she asked herself aloud. "Nobody could still be alive in there." But despite her words, she knew she wasn't ready to give up on her friends.

Elizabeth turned back to Enid. Saving her seemed impossible. Even if Elizabeth reached her friend safely, she didn't think she'd ever be able to drag Enid back past the hot wires. Still, she told herself, there had to be a way to rescue Enid without hurting her or herself. She just had to find it.

Elizabeth struggled to clear her mind, to think calmly and rationally. Instead, panic gripped her. "Jessica!" she screamed, staring wildly around her as if her twin might materialize out of the smoke.

As she watched, the wind veered slowly back to its original direction. A choking cloud once again obscured the house. Elizabeth coughed as the smells of burning wood and hot metal enveloped her. She leaned forward, her hands on her knees, until she could breathe normally again.

The choking sensation reminded her of another dark, surreal night. Her mind flashed back to John Marin, a paroled murderer with a grudge against the twins' father. Elizabeth had been going through a difficult time with Todd, and the handsome stranger who owned a sailboat and wrote novels seemed like her true soul mate. But he'd lied about everything, including his name. His real goal was to murder the Wakefield girls, to pay back Ned Wakefield for prosecuting the case that had sent Marin to prison ten years earlier.

On a dark, clear Saturday night, Marin had taken Elizabeth sailing. But he planned to return to shore alone. Elizabeth's father and sister arrived with the Coast Guard just after Marin pulled a knife on her. A few minutes later only Jessica noticed when Elizabeth hit her head while diving into the ocean to escape. She'd acted without hesitation, diving in after Elizabeth and saving her life. When Elizabeth came to, she was lying on a cot in the Coast Guard cutter, coughing up water and looking up into her sister's damp face.

No matter how terrible life got, Elizabeth reflected, Jessica seldom lost her courage, optimism, or sense of humor. She always found a way to salvage a tense situation.

This time Elizabeth would have to manage without her sister. She didn't know where Jessica was now. But she did know that Jessica was afraid, on the edge of despair. Elizabeth sensed it from the prickly feeling that was rising along the back of her neck.

She grasped her lavaliere in her hand and rubbed it with her fingers, as if it were a magic lamp. No genie appeared. Elizabeth knew what at least one of her wishes would have been. She wanted desperately to go to her twin, to comfort her and to tend to her wounds if she was injured. She wanted Jessica to comfort her as well. They were a team.

That was it, Elizabeth realized. That was the key to saving Enid's life. Teamwork. If she couldn't rescue her friend alone, then she'd find someone to help her do it.

She scanned what she could see of the back-yard.

Aaron Dallas and Max Dellon were lying unconscious near the bandstand. Dana Larson was leaning over Max, mopping his forehead with some sort of cloth. Meanwhile *Oracle* editor Penny Ayala and Elizabeth's ex-boyfriend Jeffrey French tried to revive Aaron.

Aaron started to sit up, and Elizabeth breathed a sigh of relief. She was about to call out to Jeffrey for help when she heard his voice carry over the wind. "We have to get you out of here, Aaron,"

Jeffrey said. "You're hurt pretty bad." Elizabeth watched, helpless, as Aaron, Jeffrey, and Penny staggered off.

Everyone seemed to be wounded or busy trying to care for those who were. Who would help her rescue Enid?

She suddenly thought about Todd. She longed to see him standing by her, a reassuring smile on his handsome face. No matter what—or who—had come between Todd and Elizabeth, she knew he'd risk anything to save Enid's life. But she didn't even know if Todd was alive. He had come to the party only to set things right between them. If he died because of it, she'd never forgive herself.

Terror surged through her body again, and she broke out in a cold sweat. She clenched her fists hard until the panic ebbed. She couldn't let herself think that way. *Todd's fine,* she told herself. *He probably left the party right after we said goodbye.* At this moment Enid was her first priority.

"Somebody help me!" Elizabeth screamed hoarsely. "I need help over here!" Nobody answered.

She spotted a seated figure on the other side of the pool, near the place where the barbecue had been set up. He sat hunched on the patio, his knees against his chest, and was rocking back and forth slightly, the way a small child might.

"Devon!"

Elizabeth was panting as she approached him. "Devon!" she called. "Am I happy to see you!" Of course, he'd been too freaked out earlier to be of any use. But he'd had a chance to calm down. Surely he'd recognize the gravity of Enid's plight. "Enid is in danger, Devon. I can't save her by myself. You have to help me."

Devon didn't reply. When Elizabeth looked into his eyes, she saw the tiny reflections of trees flaming hotly in the night.

On his knees in the bathroom, Todd dug into a pile of towels stored in the cabinet under the sink.

"I don't know what you expect to find in there," Lila said from her perch on the edge of the tub.

"I'm looking for something we can use to break the door," he informed her.

"In there?" Lila said. "What were you hoping to use, a lethal roll of toilet paper? Too bad Mrs. Wakefield keeps her battering ram in the other bathroom."

Todd could hear the smirk in her voice. It infuriated him. He pulled his head out of the cabinet to glare at her and was flabbergasted. In the midst of a full-blown disaster—with the house apparently self-destructing around them—Lila was calmly filing her nails.

Without knowing he was going to do it, Todd sprang forward, yanked the file from her fingers, and hurled it across the room.

Lila's eyes narrowed to their most intimidating stare. "How dare you—"

"I'm trying to get us out of here, and you haven't done a thing," he yelled back.

Lila raised an eyebrow at him. "I'm supervising."

"You're *whining*, is more like it."

Standing to face him, she poked him in the chest. She was so close that the fragrance of her perfume enveloped him like mist. It smelled expensive. "Look, Toddy boy," she said. "This whole thing is your fault, not mine. So don't give me any of your attitude."

As a general rule, Todd was not a violent person. But he knew with absolute certainty that if Lila hadn't been a girl, he would have decked her. "*My* attitude?" he yelled. "You're the one who won't lift a finger to help."

"A bonehead like you doesn't deserve my help," she said. "If you weren't such a jock brain, you'd have noticed it was a *metal* nail file you just flipped across the room." She shrugged. "Duh. Use it to pick the lock."

Todd's voice jumped an octave. "The door isn't locked, you ditz! It's *crunched* shut!"

"OK, so use the file like a screwdriver, and take the door off its hinges."

"The hinges are on the outside!" he screamed, enunciating each word. He stopped and took a deep breath, controlling his temper with difficulty. Then he returned her cold stare. Despite everything, her outfit was unrumpled and her long hair still gleamed. Why was he surprised that a girl who was so pretty was such an arrogant fool? "Fowler, do you have any idea how useless you are as a human being?"

"At least I *am* a human being and not a member of the reptile family," Lila countered. "It's easy to see why Elizabeth dumped you for Devon Whitelaw."

Todd reeled as if he'd been slapped. That was dirty. He felt his face grow hot. But he wasn't about to let Lila drag him down to her level. "If you knew anything in life beyond what shoes go with what dress," he said, "you would see that we've got better things to do right now than bicker with each other."

"And miss the pleasure of your witty repartee?" Lila said, her eyes wide and innocent. She crossed her arms in front of her and primly sat back down on the edge of the tub.

"In case you haven't noticed, those last few crashes sounded like bomb blasts," Todd said. "Most of the house must be totaled. How much longer do you think this room will last?"

"Aw, widdle Todd is scared of bad, bumpy noises in the dark," she replied in baby talk. She rolled her eyes. "Toughen up, Wilkins. We're talking about a few little cracks in the wall."

"You have a few little cracks in your head! Lila, you can't stay in denial forever."

"Don't be such a weenie," Lila replied. "You don't know how lucky you are to be stuck in here with me."

"As if!" he said with a hoot. "You just don't get it, do you? We could *die* in here!"

"Speak for yourself," Lila said with a laugh. "I have no intention of dying in a tacky little bathroom in the suburbs. Especially with *you* for company. I'm a Fowler."

"If that wall caves in, it won't stop to check your ID before it crushes you to death."

"How nice of you to care," she said acidly. "But I'm sure Daddy has already called out the Marines, the National Guard, and his private security force," Lila said. "Soon they'll show up to rescue me. And you'll be free too. So chill out!"

"Chill out?" he interrupted. "That's solid advice, coming from the original ice queen."

"In the meantime, you're much too irritating for words," Lila said. "So just stop talking to me." She spun her body so that she was facing the bathtub, her back to him.

"Stop talking to you?" Todd replied to the back of her head. "Gladly. It's the only sensible suggestion you've made."

Elizabeth shook Devon's shoulder. When he didn't respond, she dropped to her knees beside him.

"Are you all right?" she asked. "Answer me."

Devon just stared back at her blankly, as if he were catatonic. Elizabeth checked him over once again for injuries. "Devon," she said into his ear. "I know you're frightened. We're all frightened. But you've got to snap out of it now. You have to help me!"

Devon shifted his eyes and fixed on the trees that burned like torches. Elizabeth wondered what the deal was with him. He seemed to be in some sort of shock, but he didn't have the symptoms she'd learned in school. She knew Devon wasn't a coward.

She'd never seen him freeze up in a crisis. In fact, she'd seen him act efficiently and decisively.

She thought back to the night of the prom, the night she had made the mistakes that cost her both Todd's love and Devon's, probably forever. Devon had been heartbroken when he saw her dancing with Todd and knew she'd deceived him. Still, he had gathered his wits and sprung into action during the after-dance cruise party, when Todd nearly drowned.

Spoiled, vindictive Courtney Kane was the beautiful debutante who was supposed to have been Todd's date to the prom. To pay Todd back for ditching her and showing up with Elizabeth instead, Courtney had shoved him off the deck of the yacht. Elizabeth dove in after Todd. Meanwhile, Devon took charge of things on the boat, taking Courtney into custody and organizing a rescue effort.

He hadn't frozen up or given in to helplessness, Elizabeth remembered. He had figured out what needed to be done, and he'd done it. Why couldn't he do that now?

She shook his shoulder again, a little more roughly. "Devon, listen to me!" she yelled.

Devon blinked and faced her. As his eyes focused on hers, she saw a flash of recognition in them. "Enid is in trouble," she said, trying to stay calm. "She's still breathing. But she's unconscious, and she's too close to the electrical wires. We have to move now! The fire's spreading to the yard!"

Devon didn't reply, but at least he was looking at her. His expression was blank and impenetrable.

"Help me carry her to safety," Elizabeth begged. "Help me save her!"

Devon turned his head to gaze across the pool, toward the rear of the yard. Elizabeth followed his gaze and picked out Enid's form, a darker shape among dark shadows. From where Elizabeth crouched on the patio, her best friend looked heartbreakingly small and fragile.

"Please, Devon!" Elizabeth cried. "We don't have much time. Enid is going to die!"

Chapter 8

Steven pressed his feet hard against the floor-board, as if pushing would make the Jeep go faster. He wanted to urge Jessica to speed up, but the roadway was as choppy as rough seas. Jessica was negotiating its bulges and fissures as quickly as anyone could have. Probably faster than he himself would. Steven was a more cautious driver than Jessica, who liked to race down the interstate with the Jeep's top down and the wind whipping through her hair.

Steven glanced at his sister. She barely looked like Jessica. It was strange enough that she wasn't talking, but her expression was even worse. Her jaw was clenched and her eyes were grim as she squinted through the clear areas of the windshield.

Seeing his happy-go-lucky sister looking so bleak and so haunted nearly made him lose heart.

Suddenly she wrenched the wheel to the right. The tires squealed, and Steven grabbed the dashboard to keep himself from hitting the windshield. "What?" he asked, breathless.

"Oh, God," Jessica whispered at the same instant.

Steven followed her glance, and his eyes widened in horror. More than half the road was gone.

Miraculously, the streetlights along this stretch were working. Without their garish glow, Jessica never would have seen the cave-in before it was too late. The roadway had split apart, and tons of dirt, rock, and cement had swept down the bank to the left in a massive landslide that had destroyed everything in its way. The flow had roared through what used to be an apartment building at the bottom of the hill. Steven had seen that apartment complex a hundred times. Now it was just gone, erased from the landscape, as if it had never existed.

Jessica slowed the Jeep.

"Don't stop!" Steven ordered. "We have to reach Billie."

Jessica shook her head. "I'm not sure if we can. Most of the road is gone. Look how narrow it is up there. Less than one lane is left."

"We can make it," Steven said. In reality, he had no idea if they could. The Jeep just might be too wide to fit on what remained of the road. If so, they could get caught in the debris, or even slip down the hillside, following the path of the slide. But Steven was willing to take that risk. He wouldn't turn around and give up, not when Billie was less than a mile ahead.

Jessica took a deep breath and then nodded. Tears glistened in her eyes. "Let's do it." She steered the Jeep as close as she could to the far right edge of the road, practically hugging the cliff that rose above her on that side. The Jeep bounced and jostled over rocks that had fallen from above. If Steven hadn't been wearing his seat belt, he was sure his head would have been dashed against the ceiling.

"We're past it." Jessica's voice cut through the barely controlled panic in his brain. "The turn onto Main Street is just ahead."

Steven realized he'd been holding his breath. He exhaled slowly. His stomach was tied in knots. He had known this neighborhood almost as well as

123

he knew Calico Drive, but now it was utterly transformed. The slide had done much more than damage buildings. It had actually changed the locations and shapes of the streets and hills. The earthquake had gouged out a wedge of the land itself, ripped it to rubble, and cast it down the hill as easily as he might dump garbage.

He couldn't bear to think of what might have happened on Calico Drive, so he concentrated instead on finding Billie. She'd called him from a convenience store a few blocks down Main Street. As Jessica turned the Jeep onto the main thoroughfare of downtown Sweet Valley, Steven noticed, relieved, that a few of the streetlights were on, just as they'd been at the site of the slide.

As Jessica inched the Jeep along, Steven scanned the darkened businesses. Many of the buildings had crumpled like cardboard, but some were actually still standing. Jessica pulled the Jeep to a stop.

"I thought it was on this block," Jessica said, her eyes still intent on the debris-filled road. "But all the piles of rubble look the same."

People picked their way over some of the debris, dirty and vacant-eyed. Some were limping or wore bloodstained bandages. Steven's eyes searched out each figure, praying for a glimpse of Billie's chestnut hair.

"That's it!" he cried, spotting a broken sign sticking up through one of the piles of debris that had been a building only a few hours before. The sign said Drake's Mini-Mart in red-and-blue lettering.

Jessica slowed the Jeep to pull into the parking lot, but before she could turn, Steven had jumped out of the moving vehicle and was racing into the lot.

He could clearly see the cement square that marked the building's foundation. Almost nothing else was left of the store. Part of one concrete-block wall remained standing, rough and gray, its top half crumbled inward. In front of the wall sat rows of metal shelves in their usual places but dented and twisted. The merchandise that had lined them was scattered across the site and mingled with cold steel beams and soft blankets of ash. Broken glass glittered. Smoke rose from the ruins, gray and bitter-smelling, but Steven saw no flames.

Steven stared around him wildly. Then he spotted his own car, upside-down at one end of the parking lot. Steven gasped. The yellow Volkswagen Bug was flattened. If Billie had been in it when the earthquake struck, he didn't see how she could have survived.

He ran across the cracked pavement as fast as his shaky legs would carry him. When he reached his flattened car, Steven closed his eyes, clenched his fists, and tried to steel himself for what might be inside. Finally he realized there was no way he could ever be prepared. He just opened his eyes, bent down, and looked. Billie wasn't there.

Steven breathed a long sigh of giddy relief. She wasn't in the car. He sank to his knees, utterly drained.

Slowly Steven raised his eyes. If Billie hadn't been in the Volkswagen when the earthquake struck, then where was she? Heart pounding, he pivoted to look at the rubble of the store. Nothing moved among the ruins.

Horror squeezed his heart like a fist, and he shook his head in disbelief. "No!" he whispered. It couldn't be true. He would not believe that the woman he loved was dead.

Jessica was slowly stepping out of the Jeep. She'd parked it under a streetlight, and he noticed that she'd suddenly become as pale as drywall dust. She met his eyes from across the lot. Tears shone on her face.

Suddenly Steven was running, scrambling to the building's ruins as fast as his trembling legs would allow. His mind flashed on an image of his former girlfriend Tricia, gasping her final, painful breaths before the leukemia won out. "Billie!" he cried out in anguish.

Something stirred. A middle-aged Asian woman stepped out from behind the store's one remaining wall, waving a flashlight. Another woman materialized in the shadows behind her.

Steven froze, his eyes riveted on the dark figure.

"Steven!" Billie screamed. She stepped forward into the light. A smile spread across her face like a sunrise, the first smile Steven had seen in hours. They both began to run. Then Billie threw herself into his arms, and Steven swept her up in a tearful embrace.

"You're all right," he whispered into her ear. "You're all right." Her body felt warm and solid in his arms, and he wished he could hold her safe against him forever.

Devon stared at Elizabeth, his mouth hanging open. "You want me to . . . *what?*" he finally choked out.

Elizabeth began babbling something about her friend Enid, but the words seemed to run together. Only one concept stood out, crystal clear.

"You want me to go *toward* the wires?" Devon

asked, incredulous. "Go *toward* the fire? Are you out of your mind?"

Her blue-green eyes were wide with fear. She was yelling now and gesturing toward what looked like a heap of clothes underneath the back hedge, near a mess of electrical cables and spurting sparks. He heard her mention Enid's name again, but he couldn't make sense of the rest. In the back of his mind, he knew Enid was Elizabeth's closest friend. But at the moment he could hardly remember what the girl looked like.

There was a buzzing in his ears and around him, in the stones of the patio and the waters of the pool. It crawled on his skin and vibrated out from the marrow of his bones. Devon screamed.

". . . just a mild aftershock," he heard Elizabeth say. Her breath ruffled his hair, but her voice sounded distant, as if she were speaking through a bad telephone connection. A new set of fissures opened in the sides and bottom of the swimming pool, a network of thick, black gashes in the cement. The muddy water roiled, its surface iridescent and littered with floating debris.

As the vibration ceased, a cedar tree on the Wakefields' side of the fence erupted into a plume of fire, as violent as a volcano. An instant later a second cedar burst into flame. For a few seconds the wood's sweet, strong fragrance overpowered the smell of smoke. Then, as Devon watched, trembling, sparks floated down from the trees, as graceful as autumn leaves, and began to spread across the lawn.

Elizabeth's mouth was open. She was screaming something at him, but his mind was having trouble focusing on her words. "Help me save Enid!" she pleaded frantically. "Before it's too late!"

Devon shook his head. "It's already too late," he said with sudden clarity. Elizabeth winced. "The best we can do is save ourselves," he continued.

Now that his brain was beginning to work again, he recalled wanting to take refuge in the pool. He gazed into its depths and decided against it. The surface of the water looked oily now. Something must have leaked into it from one of the crevices that had opened in the cement walls and bottom. The oily water would catch fire as easily as the lawn had.

Elizabeth began to cough violently.

"We have to get away," Devon yelled into her ear. He rose to his feet and pulled her up with him. His own survival was still his top priority, he reminded himself. But he loved Elizabeth. Despite their bitter argument at the party, he knew he wanted her by his side. Some of the survivors were digging out of the yard. They'd have to make a run for that side of the house—the side farthest from the fire. "Liz, we can't wait! We have to go now!"

"No!" Elizabeth choked out the word. "I won't leave Enid!"

Devon grabbed her shoulders. "We've got to save ourselves," he yelled. "You can't help her!"

Elizabeth twisted her body away from his. She gazed across the pool at Enid, who still wasn't moving. Tears cascaded down Elizabeth's heart-shaped face. Devon longed to wipe them dry.

"You're talking about abandoning my best friend!" she screamed.

Devon shook her, hard. "And you're talking about suicide!"

Jessica burst into sobs when Billie rose from the demolished store and threw her arms around Steven's neck. Billie was alive and safe! All her suppressed fears and emotions overflowed in a torrent of tears. She ran to the couple and was enveloped in a three-way hug.

Billie and Steven were sobbing as hard as Jessica was. "Oh, Steven! When I heard your voice . . ."

After they pulled apart, Billie gestured toward

130

the woman who'd taken refuge with her behind the crumbling wall.

"You guys, this is Christine Ho, the cashier from the store," Billie said, smiling tearfully. "She followed me outside to give me my change when the quake hit. We were both out here when the ceiling collapsed."

"Thirteen cents," Christine said, her voice incredulous. "I'm alive right now only because Billie forgot to scoop up thirteen cents from the change maker."

Billie grinned. "Who said thirteen was an unlucky number?"

Jessica laughed. She knew she was on the verge of hysteria, but she didn't care. Her head was pounding from the stress and panic of the past few hours. Laughter eased the tension. For a moment she felt hopeful again.

Then, suddenly, terror seared through her body, cutting off her laughter. Her heart raced. *Elizabeth.*

Jessica was glad Billie was safe. But she had to reach her sister. She had to know if Elizabeth was all right.

"This is getting old real fast," Lila said from her perch on the edge of the bathtub.

"Bored?" Todd asked. He was sitting on the tile floor, his back to the jammed door. "Next time we're stuck in a bathroom during an earthquake, I'll hire a juggler. Or maybe you'd prefer pony rides?"

Lila looked down her nose at him. She was sick of the earthquake. She was sick of the Wakefields' bathroom. And she was totally, passionately sick of Todd Wilkins. "What about the window?" she asked, desperate for a way out. "You didn't even try to open it."

"I told you," Todd said, "it's no use!"

"Maybe for someone as useless as you."

Todd pounded a fist on the floor. "Look at that huge tree trunk that's blocking the window," he said. "We can't move the tree from in here. And there's no way either of us can fit around it to get out."

"My father says a truly visionary corporate leader believes any goal is possible."

"Ask me if I care," Todd replied. "Besides, your father never met a challenge he couldn't overcome with his platinum card."

Lila clenched her jaw. "You are so lame, Wilkins. Just because you're not bright enough, strong enough, or brave enough to find us a way out of this place, you think you can insult my family—"

Todd jumped to his feet and spread his hands.

"That's it!" he yelled. "I don't have to listen to this. If you think I'm lame, then you're welcome to take charge. Go ahead! See if you can do any better."

"Better than *you*?" Lila asked with a hoot. "That's some challenge, basketball breath. That tacky plastic soap dish could do better than you. It certainly has a higher IQ."

"Spoiled brat!"

"Nouveau riche!" She stared at him as if he were a cockroach, until he looked away. Then she rose slowly from her seat and stepped over to the small, high window. She stood on tiptoe, shifted position, and tried to peer out around the branches and leaves.

"So, Sherlock," Todd said, "has your superior Fowler mind come up with any stunning conclusions?"

Lila felt a prickly chill skate up her spine. "There's something out there," she said slowly, more to herself than to Todd.

"Now there's a blinding flash of the obvious."

Lila barely heard him. She tilted her head to gain a better view of the yard through a crook in a branch. Between the lacy network of twigs and leaves was a flickering orange light. "What's that supposed to be?" she asked aloud, her voice rising against her will. "A bonfire?"

Suddenly Todd was close beside her, jockeying

for a view out the window. His breath was warm and moist on her ear as he asked, "Where?"

Lila began to tremble. "Oh, no," she whispered. "It can't be."

"It can't be what?"

Through the window, Lila could see a corner of the Wakefield yard, on the side near Annie's house. The cedars were on fire. The lawn was on fire. And the flames were rolling inexorably toward the Wakefield house.

"Fire!" Lila screamed.

Todd jumped at the sound of her voice, so close to his ear. Lila barely noticed. She couldn't control the terror that churned inside her body. If it had been anything but fire . . .

That spring, an arson fire had gutted the west wing of Fowler Crest, including Lila's own room. She'd been home alone, dozing on the living room divan, and woke, sticky with sweat, to a room filled with smoke. Flames raced along the edges of the Persian carpet and vaulted up the damask draperies. The room blurred and tilted. And she had slipped to the floor, tiny flames flicking toward her like the tongues of snakes. . . .

Lila screamed. She wrapped her arms around her abdomen and sank to the floor of the bathroom, shivering. "I think I'm going to be sick," she said in a small voice.

Todd knelt beside her, his eyes wide with concern. Of course he knew about the fire at Fowler Crest, which had been set by John Pfeifer, the psycho who also tried to blow up the school. "No, you will not be sick," Todd said firmly.

Lila's pulse was racing. She couldn't breathe. She felt as though she were falling. She wasn't used to feeling this way, wasn't used to feeling so out of control. But the flickering orange glow had set off a terror deep inside her. Suddenly she could smell the smoke. And for the first time that night, she realized that Todd had been right: She really might die.

"We have to do something!" she screamed, grabbing his arm. "The fire's spreading this way! We have to get out of here!"

Chapter 9

Elizabeth stared at Devon, wondering if she'd ever really known him. "I can't believe you'd even suggest such a thing. How can you think about saving yourself at Enid's expense?"

Devon grasped her shoulders so tightly it hurt. "We have no choice! Do you think Enid would want you to get yourself killed?"

She wriggled out of his hold. "Enid would risk her life in an instant to save me—or to save you, for that matter. And nothing in the world will make me abandon her when she's in trouble." She grabbed his arm and gazed into his slate blue eyes. They looked strangely cold, despite the golden glow of reflected flames that now bathed the backyard. "Please, Devon," she begged in a soft, desperate voice. "If

137

you ever loved me at all, won't you help me?"

"Do I look crazy?"

Elizabeth shoved his arm away and whirled to check on Enid. The canvas umbrella in the middle of the round patio table whooshed into a shower of flames. The air was thick with ash. She wondered how long it would be before all the redwood patio furniture was on fire.

"It's spreading fast," Devon said firmly. "The house will catch soon. And then the whole backyard will erupt into one big inferno."

"I know that," Elizabeth said, her back still turned to him. "That's why we have to get Enid to safety—now!" She spun around, reached for Devon's arm, and began yanking him across the patio toward her friend.

Jessica grabbed Steven's arm and began yanking him across the parking lot toward the Jeep, trusting him to pull Billie behind him. Panic was soaring through her body, tensing every muscle and jangling every nerve. Elizabeth was facing a terrible crisis, and Jessica had a sinking feeling her sister was totally alone.

"Jessica, wait!" Steven urged.

"How can I wait when Lizzie is in trouble?"

Steven ran a hand through his brown hair, and a smudge of gray dust settled on his forehead. "Jess, I know I promised we would go to Elizabeth as soon as Billie was safe. But now—"

"What are you saying?" she interrupted. Suddenly she felt dizzy with horror. "You can't mean you'd abandon your own family!"

"No, that's just it," he said quickly, gripping her hand. "I just realized that the movie theater Mom and Dad were going to tonight is on Main, just a mile farther."

Jessica burst into tears. "Oh, God, Steven! Of course I want to find them. But Elizabeth . . . I can't! Please don't ask me to!"

Billie put one hand on Jessica's shoulder and one on Steven's. "You should go to Elizabeth," she told Jessica. "But what if Steven and I were to walk to the theater?"

Steven nodded, his face brightening. "Yes! You take the Jeep back home. We'll make our way to the theater to find Mom and Dad."

"They have the car with them," Jessica remembered.

"That's right," said Steven. "If we're lucky, it'll be in working order, and the four of us will meet you and Elizabeth back home in no time."

"What about you, Christine?" Billie asked the cashier. "You're welcome to stick with us."

Christine shook her head. "Thanks, but I'm going to try to make it home." She gave Billie a quick hug. "And thanks for forgetting your thirteen cents."

As Christine wished them luck and headed off, Jessica closed her eyes and breathed deeply, trying to calm her shattered nerves. The idea of being alone in the Jeep, in the middle of so much devastation, sent chills up her spine. She couldn't bear the thought of being separated from her brother right now. The only thing more terrifying would be remaining apart from Elizabeth while knowing her twin was in trouble.

"Jess, are you sure you're OK with this?" Steven asked.

Jessica nodded, but she couldn't force out the words to answer. Instead she threw her arms around his neck. "I love you, big brother," she whispered.

Devon jerked his arm out of Elizabeth's grasp and planted his feet firmly. She couldn't believe how stubborn and cruel he was.

"So you're really not going to help me, are you?" Elizabeth demanded.

"Only an idiot would go over there," Devon answered.

For a moment she glared at him, until the tears in her eyes blurred his face. Anguished, she spun on her heel and ran around the edge of the swimming pool toward Enid, leaving Devon behind.

The live wires still sparked and writhed with lethal current, and the pool's water pump continued to leak. Water was rising around Enid, creating a pond whose boundaries were expanding. Within minutes, the water in which Enid lay would engulf the power lines and a deadly shock would shoot into Enid's unconscious body.

Elizabeth ran as close as she dared, then jumped back when a live wire wiggled toward her like a snake. A gust of wind whipped past her, and she doubled over, coughing out a mouthful of smoke. Burning ashes streamed into the yard. And Enid was surrounded by a circle of fire. In a moment the back hedge would start to burn.

Elizabeth peered through the smoke for anyone who might help her, but she couldn't see another soul besides Devon, who stood watching her from the other side of the pool.

"Help me, Devon!" she screamed with what little voice she had left. "I can't save her by myself!"

Devon shook his head. He spoke softly, but his words carried on the wind, echoing in her ears above the roar of the fire that surrounded her. "You can't save her, period."

When Olivia awoke, she was coughing up blood. She could see the dark little blotches on the shoulder of her dress, could taste its metallic tang in her mouth. Ken was trying to smile. She knew he wanted to reassure her, but his eyes were huge and glassy. She felt terrible to be putting him through this. She didn't think she could bear to be in his position: unhurt but sitting helpless in this dusty, collapsed kitchen and watching her slowly fade from life.

As her mind gradually focused, she noticed she was seeing Ken a little more clearly than before. In fact, she was seeing everything a little more clearly. She realized there was more light. An odd glow was rippling through the air, a glow the color of peaches.

"Is the sun coming up?" she asked hazily.

Ken startled then glanced around at the reflected light. For a moment his eyes looked hopeful. Then he checked his watch, and his face fell. "No, not yet."

142

Olivia began to notice the flickering quality of the strange light. It wasn't a soft, dreamy, apricot sort of light—pastel, like a Mary Cassatt painting. It was more like a Gauguin—wild and hot, and as ferocious and free as a tiger.

"'Tyger! Tyger! Burning bright,'" she whispered under her breath, quoting a William Blake poem she'd always loved.

Burning bright.

Now she thought she knew what was causing the orange glow. And the possibility frightened her a lot more than she liked to admit.

"Livvy, did you say something?" Ken asked, his hand stroking the side of her face. "Are you in pain?"

She smiled weakly. "Not too much anymore. Mostly numb." She stopped, coughing. There seemed to be more smoke in the air. "Ken," she began after a minute, "would you do something for me?"

"Anything, Livvy. You know that."

"That light," she whispered, already weak from the effort of speaking. "That orange light."

"What about it?"

"Find out what it is."

By the time Ken returned, Olivia was sure she already knew the answer.

Ken kissed her on the forehead. "Don't worry, Livvy. It's nothing, really."

"It's not nothing," she whispered. "How bad?"

"Really, it's just some reflections." He wouldn't meet her eyes.

"The truth, Ken," she insisted. "The house is on fire, isn't it?"

Ken's eyes were red from smoke and tears. He took a deep breath, and erupted into a coughing fit. "Yes," he said finally. "A small fire is licking at the side of the house."

"How close?"

"It's on the far end of the house—the side toward Annie's, I think. We'll be safe here for a while longer," he said.

She shook her head slightly. "Not long enough for Winston to return with help," she acknowledged calmly.

Olivia watched in agony as Ken tried to hold on to his composure but finally crumbled. He buried his face in her uninjured shoulder and sobbed as if his heart was breaking. She couldn't feel the pressure of his head against her, couldn't feel the dampness of his tears through her dress. In fact, she couldn't feel her shoulder at all. The creeping numbness had claimed it. She felt her head, and a searing pain in the pit of her stomach. But the rest of her body could have been made out of cotton.

Ken's sobs subsided after a few minutes. He lifted his head and gazed into her face. He looked so desolate, she thought, with his tearstained cheeks and tense jaw. She longed to see a spontaneous smile on his handsome face, to hear his laughter one last time. But she couldn't think of a single hopeful thing to say.

She closed her eyes for a moment, to arrange her thoughts. "Ken, you have to—"

"I can't!"

"Yes, you can," she said, keeping her voice steady. "You have to get out of here."

Ken's face went pale, despite the sooty smear across one temple. "I promised I wouldn't leave you, and I won't! Not for anything!"

She was terrified of dying alone in the darkness. She wanted Ken beside her, running his fingers through her hair or cradling her cheek in his hand. She wanted to hear his deep, gentle voice, telling her over and over again not to be afraid. But it was too dangerous to let him stay with her. She had to find the words that would make him go.

"You're not leaving me," she told him as serenely as she could manage. "You're going for help. Either from Winston and the others, or from the fire department."

Olivia tried not to cough, but she couldn't help herself. Her throat felt like sandpaper. Again she tasted blood. When the coughing subsided, Ken used his sleeve to rub a spot of blood from her lip. "I can't leave you, Livvy," he said, his voice pleading. "You need me."

"But it's the only way."

The tears on his face reflected the firelight. He gazed at her, and the love in his eyes was warmer than any fire. She wanted to scream, *No, don't leave me!* But she knew she had to find the strength to let him go. It was absolutely necessary for their survival—or, at least, for Ken's survival.

Finally he nodded. "I'll be back with a whole search-and-rescue team," he promised.

"I know you will," she said. "Ken, my parents . . ." Her eyes filled with tears.

"I'm sure they're fine," he said.

"Tell them I love them," she said through her sobs. "Tell them—"

"You'll tell them yourself," Ken insisted.

Olivia nodded quickly. "I will, eventually," she said, still trying desperately to keep up her pretense. "But I might be unconscious. . . . You know."

"I'll tell them," he promised. He leaned over her and kissed her tenderly on the lips. "I love you, Olivia. I'll love you forever."

Suddenly she knew she didn't have the courage. She couldn't bear to have Ken walk away from her, to watch his lean, muscular frame as it disappeared into the flickering shadows. To be left in this horrible place, alone and scared—it was too much. Nobody could be that strong. She opened her mouth to beg him to stay.

"I love you too, Ken," was all she said.

Chapter 10

The landslide she'd skirted earlier had grown, and the rest of the road had cascaded into the canyon in another torrent of dirt and concrete. Jessica, in the Jeep, had no choice but to grit her teeth, backtrack, and find another route home.

But something else was different about this trip, she realized.

"Where did everyone go?" she whispered to herself. "It looks like a ghost town."

Jessica shuddered, wishing she hadn't thought to describe it in exactly those words. Surely there were still plenty of people in town who were alive and unhurt. They'd just gone home, or to a Red Cross shelter somewhere . . . or wherever people went when their world spun out of control.

Whatever the explanation, the lack of human activity was downright eerie. Fires raged against the horizon, while distant sirens whistled like ghosts. Overhead, jagged clouds skimmed across the surface of the moon, dappling the cratered roadway with deceptive lights and shadows. Jessica's whole body cried out with her sister's panic. But for now she had to concentrate on keeping the Jeep on the pavement.

She slowed to a crawl to negotiate a series of deep, wide fissures. Just then a person materialized out of the night, caught in the beam of her headlights. Breathless, Jessica screeched the Jeep to a halt. The figure was holding a flashlight, and the yellow beam swung wildly with his movements.

The boy ran to her window. He was about her age, with black hair and skin as starkly white as paper. Of course, she realized immediately, she was probably looking pretty pale herself. Everyone she'd seen that night seemed drained of color. Terror did that to people. He was only a few inches taller than she, but he had high cheekbones and delicate, attractive features. She thought fleetingly that he could be an actor in one of those artsy foreign films that Elizabeth liked so much.

Jessica winced as her sister's image flashed in

front of her, reproaching her for stopping. But she couldn't exactly run the guy over. She sighed, desperate to get back to Calico Drive, and rolled down her window, hoping this wouldn't take long. She left the engine running.

"I'm kind of in a hurry—" Jessica began.

"Please! You have to help me!" the boy cried, grasping the edge of the window frame with both hands. "She'll fall!"

"Hey, calm down," she urged, alarmed at his frantic tone. She flipped on her overhead light. "Now take a deep breath and tell me what's wrong."

The boy's eyes were huge and pleading, and a brilliant shade of green. His hair, chin-length and parted in the middle, swung around his face as he spoke. "I tried, I really tried! But I couldn't . . . not alone!"

"Once more, with clarity," Jessica said, her heart sinking. She couldn't leave this poor, panicky guy by himself in the middle of nowhere without at least figuring out what was wrong. But at this rate she'd never get home to her twin.

Thinking of her sister gave her an idea. Elizabeth was known as the sensitive twin, always encouraging people to talk about their problems, and helping whenever she could. She was also an expert interviewer, after all the stories she'd written for the

Oracle. She tried to remember what Elizabeth had said about how to get information out of people.

"First, tell me your name," she ordered firmly. Maybe he'd stop wigging out if he felt *someone* was in control. Personally she'd never felt so out of control in her life. But he didn't have to know that.

The boy's eyebrows arched higher over his striking green eyes, as though the question was a revelation to him. He blinked. "Bryan Hewitt," he said finally. "My name is Bryan Hewitt."

"That's a start," she said, sighing. At least his brain was beginning to kick in. "And I'm Jessica Wakefield. Now, start at the beginning and tell me what's freaking you out. The sound-bite version, please," she added. "I have to get home."

"It's my sister!" he cried. "She fell into a crevasse that opened in the ground. She's hanging on, but I can't get her out by myself. You have to help me!"

Jessica's eyes were hot with tears. She felt as if she was suffocating. "I can't!" she explained, hating herself for refusing him. "My own sister—"

Bryan reached through the window and grabbed her hand in his. "Please! She's only twelve years old."

"I wish I could help you, but I—"

"Jessica, there's nobody else nearby. She can't last much longer. You're my only hope."

Jessica squeezed her eyes shut and said a silent apology to her sister. Her stomach clenched as she tried to ignore the silent, desperate cry that had been propelling her toward her sister with such urgency. She'd never forgive herself if anything happened to Elizabeth. On the other hand, Jessica didn't even know for sure if her twin's life was in danger—only that she was frightened. How could she deny help to a twelve-year-old girl who might die without her?

"I'll do whatever I can," Jessica said, holding back tears.

She turned off the Jeep, and the engine's vibrations died abruptly. The silence crashed down around her with a terrifying finality.

Staring across the pool at Elizabeth, Devon fought an urge to call out to her that he'd do anything he could to help her save Enid's life. After all, he loved Elizabeth with all his heart, and she needed him desperately. It was his chance to show her how much he loved her. His chance to win her back.

All this flashed through Devon's mind in an instant. When he gazed across the pool at Elizabeth he could almost believe that helping her was the right decision. But everywhere else he looked, he saw reasons for sticking with his original plan of noninterference.

Enid was surrounded by flames and live electrical wires. Those dangers equaled death. Anyone with two brain cells to rub together could see that Elizabeth's friend was a lost cause. Enid could not be saved. . . .

And neither could Elizabeth, he acknowledged, if she insisted on being so pigheaded and stupid.

She took a step forward, until she was standing right at the edge of the pool, and held her arms out toward him. "Please, Devon!" she called to him. "You know it's the right thing to do."

He stared at her for another moment, and then turned away without a word.

"You coward!" she screamed.

Devon whirled. "How dare you judge me like that!" he yelled back. "What I am is a survivor!" His life hadn't been easy, and Devon knew he never would have made it this far if he hadn't been smart enough to duck out whenever the going got dangerous. "And you're nothing but a damn fool!" he added.

Elizabeth's shoulders slumped, as if she were carrying a terrible load. Devon winced slightly at the bleakness in her posture. But he couldn't allow himself to weaken. He turned away again, threw back his shoulders, and strode in the opposite direction, leaving her alone on the rim of the pool. He didn't look back.

As Devon's strong, solid form receded into the nightmarish landscape, fury poured through Elizabeth's body like a transfusion. She seldom lost her temper, but the strain of the night had overwhelmed her. Devon's cruelty was more than she could take.

"*I'm* the fool?" she shouted after him. "*You're* the one who's too stupid to see what's important in life!"

It infuriated Elizabeth to see that he didn't even turn around. She stepped forward, yelling with all her might so that he'd be sure to hear her. "Maybe it is foolish to risk your life for someone you love!" she screamed. "But if I die here tonight, I'll die next to my closest friend. You might live a lot longer than that, Devon Whitelaw. But when you die, you'll die alone!"

Elizabeth was so consumed with anger and fear, she hadn't realized she'd been inching forward as she yelled. As she stepped onto the pool's rim, one foot landed at a spot where the earthquake's force had cracked the patio, bulging it upward. She slipped on the wet surface and lost her balance, stumbling and scraping her knee as she tumbled headfirst into the filthy, oily water. She took one last, desperate gulp of air before the darkness closed in around her.

Ken burrowed under a pile of metal ductwork, broken drywall, and splintered two-by-fours. Digging his way out of the kitchen was hard work, involving a lot of climbing over piles of debris, most of them unstable. There was no clear, open path to the outside. He could only hope he'd meet up with Winston, Maria, and a team of paramedics, digging their way in.

Ken didn't know why his friends hadn't returned yet or sent help. He hadn't wanted to scare Olivia with speculation. Maybe his original assumption was correct. Maybe aftershocks really had collapsed more of the house, blocking all routes into the part of the kitchen were Olivia lay trapped. If so, it could take hours for Winston and the others to reach that spot. Now that he was alone, he allowed himself to consider another possibility. Winston and Maria might have been caught in one of those cave-ins. They might be trapped too—or worse. If they never escaped the house, then nobody on the outside knew about Olivia.

In his mind he still sat beside her, touching her curly hair and staring in awe at her beautiful, brave eyes.

He'd always known she was a courageous person. After all, it took guts to be a nonconformist. To dress differently than everyone else. To speak her mind, knowing others disagreed. To read Shakespeare on the beach while other girls leafed through fashion magazines. She'd taught him so much about being his own person, about exploring his creative side and following his hunches.

But tonight he'd learned that Olivia was much stronger than even he had guessed. She must have been petrified about lying alone and helpless in this hellish place. She had to loathe the idea of being there by herself even more than he loathed the idea of leaving her. But he couldn't argue with her levelheaded logic. She couldn't survive much longer without help from the outside.

A mouthful of acrid air set off a painful coughing fit. Ken leaned forward, his hands on his knees, until it passed. The light from the fire temporarily had improved visibility in the ruins of the house, but the increasing smoke made breathing more difficult and would soon make it hard to see. He couldn't succumb to the smoke. He had to survive and escape this place. He was Olivia's only chance.

He noticed a drawer full of tablecloths, dishrags, and linen napkins, overturned on top of a smashed piece of furniture he couldn't identify. He staggered over to it and yanked out the first piece he saw. He tied it over his nose and mouth, cowboy-style, to filter some of the dust.

Before he left her, he'd made Olivia promise she would hold on until he returned. A thin line of blood had trickled from the corner of her mouth, and he'd nearly forgotten his resolve to leave. She'd lost so much blood already. She was so weak. Did she have even the slightest chance of getting out alive, or was he kidding himself?

"No!" he said aloud to the smoke-filled cavern. Olivia was going to make it. He would return with help, and everything would be fine.

Elizabeth struggled to right herself in the foul, greasy water of the swimming pool. She couldn't see a thing. She didn't even know which direction was up. She kicked wildly. Panic seized her, and she opened her mouth too soon, gagging on a mouthful of the water. It was slick and full of grit.

Finally she broke through the surface, but something was still wrong. No random flashes of light reflected in the water. No orange fire glowed against the night. Even the moon had blinked out, like the electricity before it.

She couldn't see.

Elizabeth bobbed up and down in the water, thrashing her arms and legs. She opened her mouth to scream, but something soft was in the way. With her hands, she wiped the blobs of mud and grease from her nose and mouth, and gulped air. There was nothing to be afraid of, she told herself. It was only mud. She calmed her movements and concentrated on treading water as she wiped the filthy residue from her eyes.

When Elizabeth opened her eyes, she could see again. The water was sloshing gently around her while faint gleams of light danced on its surface. Scattered bits of debris floated nearby. Fires blazed in several parts of the yard, and the sky had an orange cast. High above, clouds ripped across the face of the moon. Everything was the way she remembered it.

Elizabeth took another deep breath, willing her hands to stop shaking. She didn't have time to panic anymore. She had to climb out of the pool and rescue her friend . . . if it wasn't already too late.

She rotated her arms, turning herself toward the rim of the pool. Then she froze, feeling the blood pulsing through her veins like a marching band. Her eyes widened, a scream dying on her lips. She was staring into the face of a rattlesnake.

Chapter 11

Todd turned away from the bathroom window and slumped against the wall, his pulse racing.

Lila's eyes widened as she looked up at him. "What?" she asked in a high-pitched voice that bordered on hysteria. "Tell me!"

Todd closed his eyes and wished he were somewhere else. Anywhere else. Lila was about to start freaking out again, he knew. And this time she might not be the only one to lose it. But he couldn't hide the truth from her forever. He took a deep breath. "The tree is on fire."

Lila jumped up from where she'd been sitting on the edge of the bathtub. "Which tree?" she whispered, taking a step toward the window. He'd never seen her so pale.

"*The* tree," he said.

She ran to the window, positioned herself to see down the trunk of the tree, and stood there, motionless. Todd stepped behind her and watched over her shoulder. Fire had leaped up from the grass below and was blazing along the trunk and dancing on the branches. Todd could see the bark blistering. The tree was right against the house, only a foot from his face. It would be only a matter of minutes before the house caught fire too.

"It can't come through the window," Lila said, her voice still squeaky and unnatural. "Glass doesn't burn, right? We'll be OK."

"Don't kid yourself. I don't know about glass, but I know that wall will burn."

"Then we'll put it out!" Lila cried, running to the sink. "We've got water. Water puts out fires. When it comes through the wall, we'll just pour water on it."

"Haven't you noticed how low the pressure is? The earthquake must have burst a water main. All we've got is the trickle of water that's still in the pipes."

"The toilet! It's full of water!"

"Lila, a few gallons is nothing. And even if we had ten times that, what would we do with it without a hose? Fill our mouths and spit it at the fire?"

162

Lila grabbed his arm and squeezed it. Her fingernails dug painfully into his flesh. "We can't just sit here and get burned up!" she screamed. "Do something!"

He wrenched his arm away. "Dammit, Lila. What do you expect me to do?"

"Break the glass! Then we'll yell. Someone out there will hear us. They'll save us."

"Break it? We could just open it," he said dryly. "But that'll only make things worse."

"No, it won't!" she wailed. "Our friends are out there. They won't let us burn in here if they know."

Todd was beginning to feel as if he were talking to a child. "The backyard is on fire. Anyone who was close enough to hear us would be out of there by now. Besides, if we open the window, the fire will blow right in here."

"Maybe not!" Lila screamed. "Maybe the wind's blowing the other way. Maybe . . ." She pounded her fists on the wall as her voice broke into hopeless sobs.

"Try to stay calm," he pleaded. "Wigging out won't do us any good."

"Neither will staying calm!" she cried through her tears. "We're going to burn up. We're going to die!" She sat on the edge of the tub again, her back to the room, and rocked back and forth like a child.

163

Todd watched her for a minute. She was so small and vulnerable-looking.

Lila Fowler? Vulnerable? he thought suddenly. Now he knew they were in desperate straits.

He tuned out her wails and stared at the window again, mesmerized by the flames. He laid a hand against the smooth windowpane. It was scorching hot. He jerked his hand away. So this was how he was going to die. Trapped in a bathroom, engulfed by fire. No, he realized, biting his lip. The smoke inhalation would probably kill them both first. Not that it mattered.

Tears were running down his face now. He wiped them away with his sleeve, but more kept coming. He'd had so many dreams. Now they haunted him like ghosts from a future he would never have. He would never reconcile with Elizabeth, would never even see her again. He'd never play college basketball, let alone make it to the NBA. He would never—

A shrill scream interrupted his thoughts. He whirled. Lila was still sitting on the rim of the tub, rocking back and forth. "Help me! Somebody help me!" she shrieked. Her voice echoed off the tiles.

"Stop it!" he yelled back, struggling to choke down his own terror. "Get ahold of yourself!" His tears turned to anger. He'd been sympathetic to Lila's fears at first, remembering what she'd been through. But enough was enough. He couldn't take any more of her hysterics. Besides, if he had to watch her fall to pieces, he'd become a basket case too. He covered the distance to her in two long strides, grabbed her by the shoulders, and shook her firmly. "Lila!" he said into her ear. "You have to stop this. Now!"

"No!" she screamed, wrenching her body away from him. "Don't touch me!" She whirled, jumped up, and ran across the room to the door. Then she pounded her fists against it, her hair bouncing wildly around her shoulders. "Help! Somebody help me! I'm trapped in here! Let me out! Let me out!"

Todd felt panic coursing through every part of his body. He didn't know what to do. It was hard enough to keep a grip on his own emotions, let alone hers. "Lila, listen to me!" His own voice seemed to come from a distance, as if he were listening to somebody else talking. It sounded shrill to him, but he couldn't control it. "Lila! Please! You have to stop screaming now. You're only making things worse."

"I'm going to burn to death!" she wailed.

"How can it be worse than that?" She pounded on the door again. "Help! Fire! Can anybody hear me? Help!"

Todd's hands were shaking. He knew how to deal with the cold, arrogant Lila Fowler. The helpless, hysterical Lila was downright disturbing. He grabbed a paper cup from the dispenser and filled it with cold water from the slow-trickling tap. He took a step toward her and threw the water at her face.

Lila's screams stopped abruptly. She stared at him, blinking as if she'd just woken up. For a moment Todd thought Lila was going to launch into one of her *how-dare-you-I'm-a-Fowler* lectures. He almost would have welcomed it. At least it would be normal for her.

Instead she crumpled to the floor, crying.

He placed an awkward hand on her shoulder. "Lila—"

"Leave me alone!" she screamed.

Todd stared out the window again, watching the encroaching flames. He was crying again, to his chagrin. The tears felt as hot as flame, searing down his face. He hoped Lila wouldn't notice. He realized suddenly that the room was hazy with smoke. What were you supposed to do in a fire? he asked himself. Shove wet towels under the crack in the door? If the rest of the house was burning, if smoke was coming in through the crack, that might help for a while. But only for a while.

Of course, Lila was in a heap on the tile, right in front of the door. He'd have to ask her to move, and she'd probably get hysterical again. Was it worth it? He didn't even know if the smoke was coming from under the door. It might be seeping in around the window.

He stared bleakly at her shuddering form, biting the inside of his cheek to keep himself from bursting into racking sobs too. If he had to die, trapped in here like a rat in a cage, why did it have to be with only Lila for company?

He remembered the spring break trip to Snow Mountain. An avalanche had thundered down the ridge, trapping him overnight in a tiny cabin with a woman named Cassandra who'd been beautiful but tiresome. As the snow buried the cabin they'd sensed its oppressive weight overhead and knew it was only a matter of time before the roof collapsed. Just before the avalanche he'd been arguing with Elizabeth. But being stuck there with Cassandra, not knowing if they'd get out alive, had made him realize how stupid his argument with Elizabeth was. She was the only person he wanted to be with, the only person he had ever really loved.

Why couldn't he have Elizabeth with him now, instead of Lila? With Elizabeth at his side, he would have the courage to face whatever came. He wished they'd never argued, wished everything could be the way it was before Devon moved to town—hanging out at the Dairi Burger, parking at Miller's Point, sitting together at football games with his arm around her shoulders.

Once, when Mr. and Mrs. Wakefield were away, Todd had spent a week staying overnight at the house. He'd thought of it as kind of a trial run for what it would be like to be married to Elizabeth, except that he slept downstairs on the couch. Of course, her parents never would have approved. He'd bought Jessica's silence by cooking for her all week and taking over her household chores. In the end, the week hadn't been very successful; neither Todd nor Elizabeth was ready for that much togetherness. But he'd always assumed that someday the time would be right for it. In his dreams of the future, it was always Elizabeth who was sharing his life.

Despair nearly overwhelmed him, and he

turned back to the window so Lila wouldn't see him cry. Having his plans and hopes go up in smoke was bad enough. But he couldn't stand the thought that he would die without telling Elizabeth how much he still loved her.

He chastised himself for wishing it was Elizabeth here with him right now. At least he knew she would live through the night. She had been outside when the earthquake struck, near the barbecue grill with Enid. Certainly she was much safer out there than in the house. The knowledge that Elizabeth was safe was like a warm, clear center of peace in the eye of the storm of fear and panic that raged inside him. At least Elizabeth wasn't feeling as scared and hopeless as he was.

"Wherever you are, Elizabeth," Todd whispered into the burning night, "I love you."

Elizabeth hung in the water, paralyzed with fear.

Her mind raced through everything she knew about snakes. Before a survival trek in Death Valley, Mr. Russo, the science teacher, had told her that rattlesnakes could swim. Elizabeth had been content to take his word for it, but now she was seeing it firsthand. And she was about to see if he'd been right about the second rule of rattlesnakes and water: that they can attack while swimming too, though not always efficiently.

What else did she remember about western diamondbacks? They were high-strung and quick to anger, she recalled. And extremely dangerous.

The snake's tongue was flicking in and out like a tiny flame, and something in the snake's posture told her it was preparing to strike.

A piece of floating debris bumped her arm. She glanced down without moving her head. It was a section of crown molding, about two feet long. *From the dining room*, she thought. But this was no time to worry about her home. Her eyes never left the snake's face, but her hand glided slowly underwater until she grasped the length of molding.

The rattlesnake pounced. As it jerked toward her Elizabeth lashed out with the stick and flipped the snake halfway across the pool. She gulped, realizing it was more than four feet long. Then she sprang away through the water, darting to the edge and hoisting herself over the slippery rim before the snake could wriggle its way back to her.

She flopped onto the patio, exhausted. She had

to catch her breath and get back to the task at hand. *Hold on, Enid,* she thought. *I'm coming.*

Jessica and Bryan stood over the crevasse where his sister had fallen. It was in the parking lot of the public library, about a block from where she'd left the Jeep. A gouge had opened up in the earth, splitting the concrete surface of the lot in wide, jagged cracks, and leaving a deep, irregularly shaped pit about four feet wide.

"She's down there," Bryan exclaimed, grabbing Jessica's arm. She could feel him shaking like a leaf.

"Get the flashlight," Jessica ordered. Bryan shone it into the crevasse. Jessica peered down, and felt as if someone had punched her in the stomach.

The flashlight beam illuminated a girl's strawberry-blond head, her tousled curls streaked with dirt. She looked up at them, and Jessica saw she had the same emerald eyes as her brother.

About eight feet below the level of the parking lot, the girl's hands gripped a small ledge, a tenuous handhold that was barely more than a bump on the rock face. At first Jessica thought the girl was suspended helplessly in the crevasse. But she

171

noticed the girl's toes were pressing down on another slim ledge, giving her a bit more stability. Her hands looked small and frail in the yellow circle of light, much too weak to hold her weight. She was whimpering.

Bryan's fingers were like a vise on Jessica's arm. His eyes were terrified, and her heart went out to him. *If Elizabeth were in that terrible, dark hole,* Jessica thought, *I'd be in hysterics.*

"What's her name?" she asked him, her voice calm but urgent.

"Alyssa," Bryan whispered, his eyes on his sister.

Panic swirled inside Jessica like a tornado, but she couldn't give in to it. She gently extracted her arm from Bryan's grip. Then she lay on the ground, her face hanging over the crevasse. "Hi, Alyssa!" she called down to the girl. "My name is Jessica. I'm up here with your brother."

"Bryan!" the girl screamed.

"I'm here," he said. His voice was shaky, but it was filled with tenderness and concern.

A few hours earlier, if someone had told Jessica that she'd be lying on her stomach in a dirty parking lot, destroying her brand-new aqua minidress, she'd have thought they were dreaming. Now she wished that *she* were dreaming. But not even her wildest nightmares could come anywhere close to the horror of this night.

"Try not to be scared," Jessica called down into the abyss, knowing it was useless advice. "We're going to get you out. I promise."

Her mind suddenly flashed on the face of her own sister, as alone and terrified as Alyssa. Every muscle in her body tensed. *Elizabeth is in danger.* The realization slammed into her like a gale-force wind. And Jessica couldn't do a thing to help her. She felt like bursting into tears, but she didn't want to frighten Alyssa and Bryan any worse. She gritted her teeth. She couldn't think about Elizabeth right now. Alyssa was here, and Alyssa needed her.

"Shine the light down past her," she told Bryan in a low voice. "I want to see how deep it is."

Bryan knelt beside Jessica. His flashlight beam illuminated the pit for what seemed to be a very long way down. It deepened into shadows without reaching the bottom.

Bryan moaned. "There's no bottom," he whispered, tears shining in his eyes. "That thing goes down forever. If she falls . . ."

"Shine the light off to the side," she told him softly. "I want to see her. But she needs to be able to look up at us without the light hurting her eyes." As long as Bryan believed he was doing something to help, she thought, she could keep him from panicking.

"Alyssa, you're doing really well," Jessica said in as reassuring a voice as she could muster. "I know your hands must be tired, but you need to keep holding on to that ledge for just a little bit longer, until we can reach you."

"I'm scared!" Alyssa said. Her soft voice was magnified by the rock walls.

"I know you are, honey," she said. "But it's gonna be all right."

Alyssa was crying in earnest now. "I'm going to fall."

"No, you're not," Bryan said. "Just pretend it's the uneven parallels."

Jessica's mind was racing for a solution to Alyssa's predicament. The girl was too far away to reach by hand, and Jessica had nothing to reach her with. There was no way of calling for help without leaving Alyssa there, and no guarantee that anyone she called would be able to come. But Jessica wouldn't give up. *I'll think of something,* she told herself. *I have to.*

In the meantime, she needed to keep Alyssa

from panicking. Thinking about normal, everyday things would help. "You do gymnastics?" she asked.

"I'm on the team," Alyssa said in a choked voice. Her face was turned up toward Jessica and Bryan.

"I used to do a lot of gymnastics," Jessica told her, trying to make her voice conversational. "I'm not taking lessons anymore, but I get plenty of practice with cheerleading. Do you like cheerleading?"

"I—I want to be a cheerleader next year," Alyssa said haltingly, "when I get to junior high." It seemed to Jessica that Alyssa understood her intent and was trying her best to do her part. *But how am I going to do my part?* she wondered. *How am I going to rescue her before she falls?*

Jessica tried to remember every earthquake news report she'd ever seen, every earthquake-preparedness tip she'd ever heard. But there had been nothing about any rescue like this.

In fact, she'd even never heard of an earthquake behaving like this. Real earthquakes didn't open up long, jagged cracks in the ground, so that people could tumble in and fall endlessly toward a bottom that wasn't there or be crushed when the rock walls slammed back together. That only happened in silly old horror movies. In real earthquakes, the big dangers were collapsing buildings and falling trees. How could this be happening to Sweet Valley?

But none of that mattered. The only thing that mattered was rescuing the girl before it was too late. Unfortunately, she didn't have the slightest idea how.

Chapter 12

Still shaking from her encounter with the snake, Elizabeth sat by the side of the pool, trying to catch her breath. She was exhausted by the lateness of the hour and the events of the night, and the gash in her forehead seemed to be bleeding again. But Enid still needed her. Elizabeth stood slowly and peered into the darkness. The water was growing deeper, the fire hotter, and the broken power lines still sparked and buzzed. Enid was in more danger than ever.

"I can't do it alone!" Elizabeth said aloud. She looked in the direction where she'd last seen Devon disappearing into the smoke, but he was gone. By now he'd probably found a way out of the yard. *I bet he's zooming away from here on his motorcycle, glad to have gotten out alive,* she thought bitterly. She had never thought Devon would be the kind of person who'd let others suffer in order to ensure his own safety. And this was a guy who'd claimed to love her.

She looked around for someone, anyone, who might help. The smoke was too thick for her to see all of the yard, but what she could see was deserted. Elizabeth had never felt so alone in her life. She had no choice. If she was going to save Enid, she'd have to do it alone.

The safest way to reach her friend was to slowly and cautiously make her way past the squirming power lines that separated them. But she'd wasted too much time already. The pool of water around Enid was growing. Soon it would reach the live wires, and Enid would be electrocuted.

Suddenly Jessica's image flashed through Elizabeth's mind. Her gut wrenched. Jessica was desperate and afraid. Elizabeth longed to help her, but she knew there was nothing she could do. Besides, she told herself firmly, Jessica was unstoppable. She knew how to act under pressure. Whatever her twin was going through, Elizabeth knew she could handle it.

"Why couldn't she be here with me now?"

Elizabeth asked aloud, her eyes on Enid's still form and the wires bristling with electricity. "Jessica, what would you do?"

She knew the answer. Jessica would throw caution to the wind. She would forget about moving slowly and carefully. She would think of nothing but saving her friend. And that, Elizabeth decided, was exactly what she herself would do.

She took a deep breath. Then she fixed her eyes on Enid and ran toward her, sidestepping the power lines that sizzled around her. She moved instinctively, dodging the danger that threatened to take her life with one misstep. When only fire separated her from Enid, she paused, catching her breath.

She had nothing with which to put out the fire and no time to figure out a plan. The flames were starting to grow, and soon they would rage out of control.

"Well, there's only one choice, then," she said to Enid, though she knew her friend couldn't hear. The fire was a narrow band. If she moved quickly, she could run right through it.

Elizabeth clenched her teeth, straightened her shoulders, and leaped through the ring of fire. She felt the heat, but her wet clothes didn't ignite. The air inside the ring of fire was hot and smoky. Enid was coughing weakly. The water was spreading. *I came through the fire,* Elizabeth told herself. *So can Enid.*

She crouched by her friend and awkwardly lifted Enid into her arms, like a child. Elizabeth's leg muscles quivered, aching, as she stood under the burden of her best friend's weight. Then she walked to the fire, staggering a bit, and passed through it.

She felt the flames lick her ankles, and once she was clear of the fire, she dropped to her knees. Setting Enid down so she was lying on her back, Elizabeth rolled over and slapped at her legs, extinguishing the flames that were singeing her socks and skin. She gasped for air. She knew she couldn't carry Enid any further. And they still had a patio full of power lines to negotiate.

At least Enid was still breathing. Elizabeth checked her pulse. Then she gently tapped her friend's cheek. "Enid!" she called. "Wake up, Enid. It's Liz! We need to get out of here!"

Enid murmured something unintelligible and then began to cough.

Elizabeth whimpered desperately. "Come on. Help me out here, Enid," she mumbled uselessly. It was clear Enid wouldn't walk out of there under her own power. But there was no way Elizabeth was giving up on her best friend. For a moment she stared at the shimmying electrical wires as if measuring up an opponent. Then she wiped the blood off her own forehead and lifted Enid's arms.

"Here we go, Enid. If you're not going to get up and walk, I'm just gonna have to drag you."

Steven and Billie stumbled into the parking lot of a strip mall on the outskirts of downtown Sweet Valley. At least, it *had* been a strip mall. Only the Plaza Theater, at the far end, was still standing. The roof had collapsed over the other stores, probably crushing everything underneath. Thin wisps of smoke or dust rose like ghosts from the rubble, glimmering in the moonlight before dissipating into the night.

Steven felt a rush of giddy relief at the knowledge that the theater was mostly intact. He squeezed Billie's shoulder. "That means they're all right!" he said with a grin.

Billie's eyes were on the toppled roof of the other stores. "I wonder how many people were in there," she said slowly.

Steven felt guilty. He'd been so glad to see the theater essentially undamaged that he hadn't stopped to think about anyone besides his parents. "The earthquake didn't come until late," he

181

reasoned. "All the stores would have been closed by then." He hoped it was true.

Billie nodded. "I bet you're right. Come on, let's see if your parents are still here."

Sudden fear shot through Steven's body. He hadn't thought about it until now, but why would his parents still be here? Surely nobody would stay at a movie after a major earthquake. They would speed home to their children, wouldn't they? If his parents were here, that meant they were hurt. He froze, his fists clenching and unclenching at his sides.

Billie turned to see why he wasn't following her. She looked taken aback when she saw the expression on his face. "I bet they're on their way home right now," she assured him. "But we have to check."

Steven nodded. "Right," he said quickly, focusing on her confident eyes.

"The car!" Billie exclaimed. "The only cars in the parking lot are in front of the theater. Let's see if your folks' car is still here."

Steven broke into a run. The moon was shining, free of the clouds, and it bathed the parking lot in a soft glow. He scanned the rows of cars. His heart dropped. "I see Dad's car," he said in a flat monotone. *Please don't let my parents be hurt,* he begged silently.

"Maybe they're fine, but they left the car because it was damaged or something," Billie suggested as she took his hand and led him toward the building.

"I don't know. It looked all right to me," Steven said.

"Could they have found another way home?"

Steven thought that was unlikely. But he couldn't dwell on all the unthinkable possibilities that were flitting through his mind. The first order of business was to check inside that theater.

"Rope," Jessica said to Bryan as they sat at the top of the crevasse where his sister was still trapped. "The one thing we could really use right now, short of the fire department, is a good, strong piece of rope."

Bryan nodded. "Do you have any in your Jeep?"

Jessica shook her head. "No such luck. The Jeep's brand-new. My parents gave it to my sister and me for our birthday, just tonight. . . ." She stopped, annoyed to find tears overflowing her eyes all of a sudden. "Sorry."

Bryan put a hand on her shoulder. "You said you had to go somewhere. Your family?"

Jessica wiped away the tears with her hand.

"They'll be OK," she said. "It's Alyssa we need to worry about now. And there's nothing useful in the Jeep."

"Well, what else can we use?" he asked, his hand on his forehead.

"Do you have a car nearby?" Jessica asked.

Bryan shook his head. "I was walking Alyssa home from a party when the earthquake hit. I didn't have anything with me but a flashlight." Tears pooled in his eyes. "She doesn't like walking in the dark."

Jessica lay on her stomach again. "Hey, Alyssa!" she called in her most cheerful voice. "Don't you worry. Your big brother and I are cooking up a rescue scheme right now. Can you hold on a little bit longer?"

"Yes, I will," Alyssa said, whimpering softly.

"You're really good with her," Bryan said. "I'd be a total basket case by now if you hadn't come along."

"We need something we can use instead of rope," Jessica said. "Something we can lower down to her. Any ideas?"

"Too bad neither of us is wearing jeans," Bryan said, picking at the hem of his khaki shorts. "We could've tied them together."

Jessica raised her eyebrows. "That would have been a really good idea," she said, impressed. "I should've worn bigger clothes." She looked around the lot for something else that might work.

"Our belts!" Bryan cried, snapping his fingers.

Jessica almost hugged him. "Yes!"

Her new minidress had come with a narrow leather belt, dyed to match the blue-green color. She whipped it out through the belt loops and held it up triumphantly. "Give me yours." She buckled the belts together and yanked on them. "They seem strong enough. Let's try it."

"Alyssa, it's Jessica," she yelled, plopping herself down on her stomach again so she could lean into the fissure. "Remember I told you Bryan and I were thinking up a plan? Well, here it is."

Jessica held the flashlight while Bryan lay down beside her. He dropped one end of the makeshift rope into the hole while explaining to Alyssa that she should grab it with one hand.

"I can't!" Alyssa wailed.

"I know it's scary, taking one hand off the wall," Jessica said. "But you do it on the uneven bars all the time, don't you? You're a brave girl, Alyssa, and you're strong. You can do it."

Alyssa shook her head. "It's not that. I can't reach it. It's too far away."

"Damn," Bryan said aloud. Alyssa's face pivoted upward, her green eyes wide and terrified.

Jessica pursed her lips and shook her head at Bryan. They had to stay calm and confident in front of his sister. "It's all right, Alyssa," she said quickly. "We'll just find a way to make our rope longer."

"We need longer belts," Bryan said. Every line of his body was etched with tension. He was breathing so heavily that she was afraid he would hyperventilate.

"I never thought I'd be saying this to any guy I was with, but I sure wish you and I were fatter."

"Bryan! Jessica!" Alyssa called up the shaft, her voice tearful but brave. "I'm scared."

"It'll be OK, honey," Jessica called. "You know how it is in the movies—when Plan A doesn't work, you go to Plan B. We're working on Plan B now." She searched for a subject of conversation to keep Alyssa's mind occupied. "Tell me about the party you went to tonight. Was it a birthday party?"

"An end-of-sixth-grade party," Alyssa said. "My friend Sarabeth gave it at her apartment."

"I had a party tonight too. Mine was a birthday

186

party. My sister and I turned seventeen today. No, I guess that was yesterday by now." Jessica barely noticed what she was saying. Her mind was too busy racing through rescue options and discarding them.

"My hands hurt," Alyssa wailed. "I can't hold on much longer."

Jessica looked at Bryan. Her own terror was reflected in his clear green eyes. He shook his head to let her know he hadn't thought of anything. Neither had Jessica. She still didn't have a single workable solution for getting the girl to safety.

She dropped her voice so Alyssa wouldn't hear her. "We have to think of something, Bryan. Fast."

Ken spotted the butcher block table that Maria and Annie had been hiding beneath. Even its sturdy construction hadn't held up indefinitely. The last series of aftershocks had dumped the rest of the second floor onto that side of the kitchen. The table had collapsed beneath a heavy section of roofing. Its legs, a few sticks of light-colored oak, jutted out from one side of the heap.

Ken doubled over, coughing from the smoke. He was beginning to feel dizzy. But he couldn't worry about that now. He had to get out and bring back help for Olivia. For a moment he thought he heard voices. He stopped to listen, but decided he'd imagined it. *Great. Now I'm hallucinating,* he thought.

Olivia was counting on him. She needed him to keep his head clear. He straightened the linen napkin he still wore over his nose and mouth. He looked around carefully, fixing in his mind an image of the Wakefield kitchen as it had looked before the earthquake. Then he took a few steps to the right, until he was sure he was standing at the exact spot where the sliding glass doors had been.

Of course, the glass doors themselves would be in fragments now, he realized, probably under a stack of drywall. But part of the opening for the doors had been clear enough for Winston to crawl through. Maybe he could find Winston's crawl-space.

A few minutes later he thought he was in the right place. There was no clear exit, but if he could move away some of the wreckage, he might find a way out. A battered bookshelf he recognized from Elizabeth's room lay across his path. He tried to lift it and was surprised when he couldn't.

What's wrong with me? he wondered, feeling

more and more frazzled every minute. He was a football player, and he was in good shape. The smoke inhalation was affecting him, he thought. Or pure exhaustion. It was well past midnight, and he'd never been so tired in all his life. Still, there was no way that he would rest comfortably until Olivia could. He finally wrenched the bookshelf out of the way.

Ken was coughing so hard he could hardly stand up straight. But he had to keep going. He pawed through piles of battered books and came to a heavy piece of pipe. It was blocking his way. He pulled it with both hands, but it wouldn't budge.

"Dammit! This is taking too long!" he cried. He could see flames already licking at various parts of the wreckage around him. He needed to get Olivia out of there and to a doctor. There was no time for digging through the fragments of everything the Wakefields owned.

He grabbed at the pipe and yanked it again. It loosened suddenly and came out in his hands, sending Ken sprawling backward. Pulling out the pipe disturbed a pile of other debris. There was an ominous creaking sound, and then a snapping. Dust and fragments of drywall cascaded down in a fine shower. Ken turned away, protecting his eyes with one arm until the dust settled. When he looked up, cool air blew against his face. It could only have come from outside. He'd found the way out.

He stuck his head up through the gap in the wreckage and didn't see a single person in the backyard. Of course, he could hardly see any of the backyard. The smoke out there wasn't as thick as it was inside, but it was thick enough to hamper visibility. Fire reflected in it, turning the night a murky orange-gray.

"Is anybody out there?" Ken hollered as loudly as he could. He stopped, coughing. "Help!" The hole was only about as wide as his shoulders, but he was pretty sure he could fit. He pulled the cloth napkin down off his face. Then he stuck his head and arms into the gap and began squirming through it, yelling for help as he did.

"Ken?" came a girl's voice through the smoke. "Ken, is that you?"

"I'm crawling out of the house," he called back. "Can you see me?"

A tall figure materialized through the tawny smoke. It was Maria Slater. Her ebony face and short black hair were gray with dust. She was staggering a little, and there was a nasty bump on the side of her head. "Are you hurt?" she asked as she helped pull him out of the rubble.

He shook his head, trying to catch his breath. "Not me . . . Olivia!" he said, gasping. "Trapped in the kitchen, under a big beam, the refrigerator . . . She's hurt bad." He grabbed Maria's shoulders. "And it's burning in there."

"Out here too," Maria said. "Almost everyone's hurt."

"What about Jessica and Elizabeth? And Todd?" he asked, his breath coming more easily now that he was outside, though the smoke still seemed to scrape against his raw throat.

Maria shook her head grimly, then raised her hand to her temple as if the motion had hurt her. "I haven't seen them," she said.

Ken turned back to what was left of the house. From this vantage point, it was hard to believe that anyone inside could still be alive. "Todd was inside before the earthquake," he said, his jaw tight. "But I've been in there for hours, and I haven't seen him since before it hit." With a wave of horror, he realized that Todd Wilkins was probably dead. Who knew where Jessica and Elizabeth were?

"Oh, God. I can't take much more of this," he cried, feeling his resolve start to shatter.

"Come on, Ken," Maria said calmly, reaching out to touch his shoulders. "Keep it together."

Ken swallowed back the pain and loss and struggled to get a grip on himself. "We have to get help for Olivia!" he said quickly. "It'll take at least four strong people to pull her out of there."

"I doubt we have four strong people. I was knocked out for a while, but Maria Santelli just found me and she said a lot of the kids went home to their families. Some of the others are in no shape to help. Winston's out front trying to find someone to help dig you out. They couldn't get back through to you." Tears began spilling from her eyes. "Ken, we thought you were dead."

"I'm fine, Maria. It's Olivia we should be worried about. Let's go try to help Winston." Ken took Maria's arm and started to walk around what was left of the house.

"Ken, you should know that all the phones in the neighborhood are out," Maria said calmly. "This is a lot bigger than just Liz's house. There are fires in the distance, and we've been hearing sirens nonstop, and houses and trees crashing . . ."

"So we might not be able to find anyone," Ken said slowly. He looked back at what was left of the house. Olivia was in there. Alone. Scared. Fading fast.

"I understand what you're saying, but we don't have much more time. I have to *do* something, Maria, no matter how hopeless you think it might be." He started to rush, pulling Maria along with him.

As they left the backyard Ken looked behind him. A breeze blew through the yard just then, fanning the flames and spreading them but also clearing the smoke for a moment. In one quick glance, he took in the catastrophic scene. The house was in shambles. Miraculously, one window was actually intact in one of the few sections of wall that were still standing. A tree had fallen across it, and the tree was on fire, burning like a Roman candle. The wall near the window was beginning to smoke.

In the yard, fires were breaking out everywhere. Maria Santelli was helping Dana Larson carry an injured boy away from the demolished bandstand. By the side of the pool, he saw one girl leaning over the crumpled form of another while broken electrical wires showered sparks nearby. He couldn't recognize either girl at this distance.

Ken couldn't believe what he was seeing. The destruction was total, as bad as any footage on the evening news about bombings in distant, war-torn countries. But this wasn't on the other side of the world. It was his own Sweet Valley. And in the middle of it all, his Olivia lay helpless, crushed beneath a pile of rubble.

"We'll find help," he said under his breath as they raced toward the front yard. "We have to."

Chapter 13

Lila slumped with her back against the bathroom door, grimly contemplating her death as tears streamed down her face. She would never graduate from high school, would never have the most awesome dress at the senior prom. She'd never gamble in Monte Carlo or plan the wedding of the century for six hundred guests. She'd never even get to say goodbye to her parents. Or to Jessica or Amy.

"Oh, no," she whispered under her breath. For the first time it occurred to her that her parents and friends could be dead. She began to sob. She'd been so worried about her own situation that she hadn't stopped to think of anything beyond the four walls that seemed to be closing in around her and Todd.

Todd. What a cruel stroke of luck. But there he was, sitting on the edge of the tub, where she'd been earlier. Dying with Todd was worse than dying alone. Todd didn't care at all about her. Sure, he'd been nice to her a couple of times that night. But only for a few seconds. And only, she decided, because he was sick of listening to her cries and was desperate to make her stop.

In truth, there were very few people she'd want to have with her as she died. She had tons of friends. But only Jessica—and Amy, to an extent—felt like *close* friends.

When John Pfeifer had tried to rape her on a date at Miller's Point, most people at school had believed John's story instead of hers. After all, he was the sports editor of the *Oracle*. He was steady, solid, and dependable. A nice guy. And everyone knew Lila as a flirt who liked to dress in sexy clothes and date a different guy every weekend.

Some of Lila's friends had stuck by her. But Jessica was the only one who knew her well enough to guess that something was wrong, a whole week before Lila reported the assault. It was Jessica who'd showed up at Fowler Crest and barged into Lila's room to check on her. It was Jessica who'd helped her come up with a plan for

196

making sure everyone knew the truth about John.

Lila had been vindicated since then, as John had gotten his revenge for his ruined reputation by torching first Fowler Crest and then Sweet Valley High. Now everyone knew how troubled and violent he'd been. But Jessica hadn't waited for proof. She had believed Lila's version of events from the very beginning. If Jessica's best friend said it had happened, then that was good enough for Jessica.

The two argued a lot. The rivalry between them was intense. But in the end, they always stuck together. Jessica had even forgiven her for the time Lila took her on a trip to Jamaica without telling her that they were there not as tourists but as counselors to a bunch of kindergarten brats.

Then there was the time they'd nearly scratched each other's eyes out when they both fell for Lucas, a ski instructor at Snow Mountain. But Jessica and Lila had stuck together and consoled each other when the no-taste jerk decided he liked Enid Rollins better than either of them.

Unfortunately, Jessica was an exception. An aberration, even, Lila told herself ruefully. Other people hung around because they liked being seen with her, Lila Fowler, who was not only the richest girl at school but one of the most attractive and impeccably dressed. Probably some of them really did like her. Maybe they'd even wanted to get to know her better. But Lila held the world at a distance, keeping herself apart from other people. And in the Fowler vocabulary, "apart from other people" meant "above other people."

What good had all that snobbery done her? None at all, she realized. With a fiery death flickering against the window, her superior attitude seemed downright pointless.

A sharp noise, like a gunshot, made Lila jump. Todd looked up too. The windowpane had cracked from the heat.

This was it. The fire and smoke would rush in very soon now, and she and Todd would die.

Lila buried her face in her arms and dissolved into sobs of self-pity, despair, and loneliness.

The Plaza Theater was an old-fashioned movie house that specialized in classic films. Steven knew the building was an old one. His mother's design firm had helped with the interior renovations. So he was surprised, but grateful, that the building had held up so well.

"Looks like the only real damage is in front," Billie said.

Steven nodded. The stucco-covered brick facade had crumbled off the building and lay on the sidewalk in piles several feet deep, blocking the entrance. The marquee had fallen there too, twisted but intact. Large red letters spelled out Now Playing: *Henry V*.

"The place seems deserted," Billie said. "That's odd, with so many cars still here. But we can't even get close enough to the doors to see."

Steven bit his lip. He had to concentrate on solving each problem as it came up. If he thought too much about what he might find if they finally got inside, he'd never make it. "Theaters have emergency exits," he said. "Maybe the side door isn't blocked."

"I'll go check it out," Billie said. "Why don't you see if you can find a way in here?"

Steven nodded. After Billie hurried around the corner, he cupped his hands around his mouth and yelled toward the double doors as loudly as he could. "Hello! Is anybody in there?"

His heart nearly stopped when he heard a response. People were pounding on the inside of the doors and shouting. Steven couldn't make out the voices, but he hoped his parents' were among them.

"It might take a while, but we'll get you out!" he called, just in case they could hear him better than he could hear them. He dropped to his knees and began clearing away bricks.

"The side door is blocked even worse," Billie said when she rejoined him a few minutes later. "Part of the roof next door fell against it."

"People are trapped inside," he said, keeping his voice calm with some effort. "They were pounding on the doors."

Billie knelt beside him and helped him lift a heavy section of bricks that were still mortared together. "Your parents?"

"I don't know. I couldn't hear them well enough to ask, but it sounded like a lot of people."

"Don't worry. We'll find them." Billie glanced first to the marquee and then at the mound of rubble. Then she rolled up her sleeves and quoted from the Shakespeare play, "'Once more into the breach!'"

Steven laughed, glad to have Billie by his side. He felt terrible for all the people who must be going through this night away from the people they loved the most. Especially his sisters.

Jessica felt self-consciousness, an unfamiliar emotion for someone who relished the limelight as much as she did. But her fear for Alyssa's safety was stronger than her discomfort. If saving a young girl's life meant letting a boy she barely knew hold her by the legs as she dangled upside-down in a crevasse while wearing a short dress—well, then that was what Jessica would do. Luckily, the dress was a stretchy fabric that hugged her body like a bathing suit. She hoped it would stay put instead of riding up and collecting around her waist.

Of course, Bryan couldn't hold the flashlight while holding Jessica. He probably couldn't see her anyway, she reasoned, even though he had a powerful hold on her knees. Not that he was thinking about anything but rescuing his sister.

"Hang on a few more minutes, Alyssa," he yelled.

"I've almost got you," added Jessica. She knew that she was doing something incredibly danger-ous. If Bryan lost his grip on her, even for an in-stant, she would plunge into the bottomless crevasse, probably taking Alyssa with her. She shuddered, wondering if he could feel the goose bumps rising on her legs.

Alyssa's bone white hands seemed to glow against the dark rock they clung to. But after the first few feet, everything else in the fissure was as dark as the bottom of the ocean. And nearly as cold. The tomblike dampness was already working its way into Jessica's skin. She hated to think of how uncomfortable Alyssa must feel.

She remembered being cold and wet in the basement of the cheerleading advisor's home when the delusional woman had taken her and the other cheerleaders hostage. They'd been bound and gagged and petrified. But with Elizabeth's help, the whole squad had managed to escape. This time Elizabeth was nowhere near. *At least I'm not alone,* she thought. Bryan's hands on her legs felt surprisingly strong.

"Are you anywhere close to her?" he called down.

"Not yet. You'll have to let me down a little farther so I can reach her—see if you can work your way lower on my legs, until you're holding my ankles." Her own voice sounded oddly hollow. She wasn't sure if the distortion was caused by the echoing rock walls or the horror in the pit of her stomach.

"It's a good thing you're a trained gymnast," Bryan said.

"It's a good thing you've got strong hands," she replied, trying to quell the hysteria that was rising within her. Her own fear and Elizabeth's seemed to have merged. She could no longer distinguish between them.

"Jessica!" Alyssa screamed. Her voice reverberated like a reproach. "Help me! The rock's getting all crumbly."

Jessica felt a tiny jerk, like an electric spark, flash between Bryan's hands and her own skin. For a moment she was sure he was about to panic and drop her.

"Sorry," he said, his voice tight and small.

"What rock, Alyssa?" she asked. She held her breath.

"The bumpy place I'm holding! Jessica! Help me!"

Bryan's hands were on Jessica's ankles now.

"I've almost got you, baby," Jessica yelled to her. "Bryan, lower me just a bit more. Can you lean in a little?"

Jessica stretched her arms as far as they would go—and felt her fingers graze the young girl's cold hands. "A little more, Bryan. I can touch her, but I can't grab—"

"I'm slipping!" Alyssa screamed suddenly. One of the small hands moved on the rock ledge. "Jessica! Save me!"

❖   ❖   ❖

Lila felt a hand on her shoulder. She looked up to see Todd kneeling beside her. This time he didn't look exasperated and condescending. In the dim light from the candle on the toilet tank and the blaze outside the window, she could see his big brown eyes. They were dark with concern.

"I'm scared too," he said in a choked-up voice. "I didn't want to let you see it. I was too embarrassed. But that seems silly now."

Lila nodded, tears still hot and wet on her cheeks. A lot of things seemed silly now that she was about to die. She began to cough—harsh, painful barks that seared her throat. Todd's hand tightened on her shoulder. "You OK?" he asked when she was able to catch her breath.

Lila nodded again. For once in her life she couldn't think of a single word to say. Besides, talking hurt her throat. She was just grateful for Todd's steadying hand. More than anything, she was afraid of being alone.

"I don't want to die alone," he said.

Lila gasped. He'd known exactly what she was thinking, as if he'd read her mind. Without planning it, she threw her arms around him, weeping bitterly into his shoulder. Todd clasped his own arms around her back and held her tightly, rocking back and forth. And Lila was shocked to realize that she actually felt secure in his embrace.

Elizabeth had been holding Enid by her hands, but dragging her that way was becoming awkward. She stopped to shift position, grabbing Enid under the arms, from behind, with her hands clasped just below her friend's collarbone. They had only another few feet to go before they would be clear of the exposed power lines.

Elizabeth was walking backward, dragging Enid along behind her. As if her own fear wasn't enough, she was aware again of fear from Jessica—fear that was rising rapidly to terror. For an instant it shook her whole body. Despite the warm night and the heat of the fires, Elizabeth was suddenly cold. Goose bumps bristled on her legs. But she pushed the fear away.

Then, out of the corner of her eye, Elizabeth glanced down. One of the live, sparkling wires was lashing toward her ankle.

The world seemed to shift into slow motion as the power line glided toward her, undulating like a snake in water. It trailed sparks that painted a white-light afterimage on the air, as bright as neon. Elizabeth longed to run, to escape to safety, but her feet were rooted to the pavement. Besides, she couldn't move with quickness or agility without dropping Enid and leaving her to the mercy of the uncaring current. With sick dread rising in her stomach, Elizabeth watched the glittering wire flying at her and realized how utterly helpless she was.

Sizzling pain sliced through her ankle, jerking her entire body. Elizabeth slumped to the ground, beside Enid, jittering. She'd never felt such pain, and it wasn't stopping. She heard screaming. It was coming from her own mouth. The electricity coursed through her legs, jolted up and down her spine, more violent than the earthquake. It was cold and hot, fast and slow. She couldn't think, couldn't move.

Fleetingly Elizabeth ordered herself to hold on to consciousness. She remembered something about a fire. She didn't know what the fire had to do with the pain. But if she passed out, she knew that she and Enid would die. The world was shaking. Or Elizabeth was shaking. It didn't matter. She couldn't see, couldn't breathe. Then everything faded to gray.

Chapter 14

Ken heard Maria's labored breathing behind him as he rushed into the road. Vaguely he noticed other fires burning all along Calico Drive. But his attention flew to the fire department rescue truck that was jostling toward them on the bumpy, furrowed roadway. As if on cue, the siren blared, swelling to fill the night. Its flashing lights burned through the smoky haze that hung over the neighborhood.

Ken felt a rush of euphoria. He was still worried sick about Olivia. But he wasn't alone anymore. Adults were here now—experts who could take over the life-or-death decisions. For the last few hours he'd felt as if he were drowning in the responsibility of it all.

He stood in the road and waved his arms desperately. The truck shrieked to a stop in front of the Wakefield house. Inside were four brawny men and a muscular blond woman as tall as Ken. One man wore a uniform with an EMT badge. The others were dressed in firefighters' clothes. Ken ran to the driver's door.

"This the Wakefield house?" the man at the wheel asked. He had broad shoulders, fiery red hair, and a sympathetic face.

Ken nodded frantically. "She's trapped inside. You have to help her! She'll die!"

The man consulted a clipboard as he climbed from the truck. His colleagues began unloading equipment at lightning speed. "That's Olivia Davidson, sixteen years old?"

"That's right," Maria replied. Ken noticed she was leaning against the truck for support. "How did you know?"

"A kid named Egbert ran into the station a while ago and ordered us to get over here or else."

Ken silently blessed Winston for coming through. "Olivia's hurt badly," he told the man. "But there's heavy stuff on top of her. We couldn't get her out. I can lead you right to her."

The red-haired man gazed at the house. "I'm

not sure about this. Egbert didn't say the whole place was in flames."

"It wasn't yet when he left," Ken said, fighting the urge to grab the rescuer by the hand and drag him to Olivia's side.

"Normally we'd send a hook-and-ladder as a matter of course," the man said. "But the whole town's in ruins. There wasn't one to spare."

"Should I call in for instructions?" asked a dark-haired Latino man in his early twenties, reaching into the truck for the two-way radio.

"That's affirmative, Victor—" the first firefighter began.

"Instructions? What instructions?" Ken shrieked. "What do you need to know? Just go in there and get Olivia out!"

"Calm down, son. We're a search-and-rescue team. We can pull your friend out of the wreck-age and stabilize her for transport. But this vehi-cle's not equipped for fighting a full-blown blaze."

Finally the stress of the night overwhelmed Ken. White-hot fury raged through his body, and he couldn't hold back for a second longer. He felt as though he were watching himself from above as this out-of-control Ken stranger reached out and grabbed the rescue worker by the collar of his fire-resistant coat.

"I don't care what you're equipped for!" Ken yelled. "She needs your help! You're going to save her, and now! Or I swear I'll pound you to a pulp."

"If Ken doesn't, I will," Maria added, waving a fist. She looked too dizzy to stand, let alone fight.

Two of the crew had rushed to their team member's aid at the first sign of trouble, but the man held up a hand to stop them. "Relax, everyone," he ordered. His calm, measured tones cut through Ken's hysteria, and Ken dropped his grip on the man's collar. "We'll do everything we can to get your friend out."

"I asked for a hook-and-ladder," Victor reported. "Could be some time, though."

The redheaded man looked at Ken and nodded. "Then we'll manage with what we've got."

Steven and Billie pushed their way through the crowd that began streaming from the theater entrance as soon as the two had pushed away the last of the debris and opened the double doors. Inside, the emergency lights cast a dull, golden glow. Steven scanned the faces of the rushing people. Some seemed stunned, but most just looked relieved. He didn't see the two faces he was searching for.

"Please be here," he repeated under his breath, over and over again. Billie squeezed his hand.

Suddenly Steven spotted a head of hair exactly the same shade of brown as his own.

"Dad! Over here!" He began threading his way through the running people, pulling Billie behind him. Yes, there was Ned Wakefield, all right. His arm was wrapped around his wife's shoulders as they hurried toward the doors. They both looked exhausted but unhurt. "Dad! Mom!" Steven yelled again, trying to attract their attention.

At exactly the same moment their faces turned toward him and Billie. They brightened with relief, and Mrs. Wakefield's eyes grew wet. A moment later the four were hugging as if they'd never be parted again.

After a minute his father took a deep breath and turned to Steven. Lines of tension Steven had never seen before creased his forehead. "Your sisters?"

"I was out with Jessica when it hit," Steven said quickly. "I saw her not long ago. She was fine."

"As far as we know, Liz is at your house," Billie

211

added as they walked out of the building. "But we haven't been back there."

"Then that's where we're headed," said Mrs. Wakefield, stepping gingerly over the bricks that littered the sidewalk on both sides of the entrance. Her voice was calm, but stress had carved deep grooves at the corners of her mouth.

"There were no injuries in the theater?" Billie asked.

"Luckily, no," Mr. Wakefield replied. "No damage at all."

"But the movie was really something," his wife said wryly. "I never knew that battle scenes could be so realistic."

Steven remembered the first, terrifying rumbles that had signaled the start of the nightmare. He shuddered. That seemed like weeks ago, but it had been only a few hours.

As the four walked to the car, Steven noticed the sky. It was glowing softly with the first faint glimmers of dawn.

Elizabeth tried to open her eyes and could not. She didn't remember where she was or what had happened. Her muscles ached horribly. Her brain felt fried. She was hot and cold at the same time. She heard a sizzling noise that she knew was power lines, but she couldn't recall why she knew.

The fuzzy grayness washed over her again. Elizabeth began to drift in it. But anguish slammed into her, red and black. Anguish so intense it was a physical pain, a spasm of grief and horror worse than any of the other aches that sliced through her body. She saw a face in her mind. . . .

Jessica. Elizabeth's brain formed the word, but her mouth couldn't say it. But that couldn't be right. Jessica wasn't here.

The world was moving, she noticed vaguely. Was it another earthquake? No, she was the one who was moving, not the earth. Someone was carrying her. She didn't know who. But her eyes wouldn't open, and her mouth couldn't form the words to ask. She remembered Devon. She had wanted him to help her with something, but he wouldn't. He went away. Had Devon come back? Or was it Todd? But nobody had seen Todd.

She was drifting again, like floating in the pool. Then a snake lurched toward her, and she was startled awake. There was something else she had to remember. Something about Enid and a ring of fire . . . *I have to save her,* she thought. But it was too hard to concentrate.

She relaxed and let the darkness consume her.

"I'm slipping!" the terrified girl cried. "Jessica! Save me!"

Jessica was dangling from her ankles, just above the girl. Her eyes were fixed on Alyssa's face. Her fingertips grazed one of Alyssa's small white hands—hands that were losing their grasp on the tiny, crumbling ledge.

"Lower, Bryan!" Jessica shrieked. But Bryan was already leaning as far into the pit as he could. His grip tightened on Jessica's ankles.

"Alyssa!" he screamed.

"Jessica!" shrieked the young girl. As Jessica watched in horror, the ledge broke away from the rock face. Alyssa's small white hands disappeared from view, but her wide green eyes caught a gleam of light, boring into Jessica's as the girl plummeted down into darkness.

Jessica shut her eyes to block out the devastating sight of those terrified green eyes. But she couldn't shut out the sound of the girl's voice. Alyssa was screaming—one long, continuous, wordless shriek of horror and helplessness.

Jessica felt a jerking motion from above as Bryan reeled. His fingers dug harder into her ankles. Suddenly Alyssa's scream was cut off with sickening abruptness.

"No!" Jessica howled. Her voice reverberated off the walls of the fissure, bouncing and echoing in the dark. There was no reply.

Chapter 15

The fractured bathroom window gave way, shards of glass suddenly popping from the frame. They must have made a noise, Todd thought, falling like that. But the roar of the fire overpowered it. The flickering orange flames licked along the inside edges of the wooden frame and crept into the room like a cat burglar. Lila screamed.

Todd stood in the middle of the bathroom, his arms wrapped around her, and stroked her hair to calm her. He sighed with resignation. This was it. The bathroom was burning. A few narrow tongues of fire began to steal along that wall. Soon the other walls would burn too.

He hugged Lila tighter. "We should get in the bathtub," he said into her ear. "Buy us some time." The bathtub was at the opposite end of the room, and somehow he felt the ceramic would protect them. Todd didn't know what good the few extra minutes would do. And of course the tub wouldn't save them from smoke inhalation. But it was the kind of thing you learned to do in safety courses—a lesson you always assumed you'd never need.

Together they climbed into the tub and sat there, holding each other tightly. "I have to tell you something," Lila said, her voice hoarse. "I never really liked you."

Todd laughed. Even to himself, his laughter sounded a bit hysterical. *Lila never liked me.* That was no surprise. And what a thing to worry about at a time like this!

"I'm serious," she said. "I wish I'd been nicer to you all these years. . . ." Her voice broke into a spasm of coughing.

"Don't try to talk now," he whispered.

"Why not?" she asked roughly. "What am I saving it for? Besides, I want you to know . . ."

The smoke was in his throat, in his lungs. He choked on it as if he were drowning. Lila pounded him on the back. "Todd?"

He nodded. "I'm OK."

"I don't want to die," she whispered, her body shuddering with fear. "But you're a good guy. If I have to die, this wouldn't be such a bad place. . . . I mean, with you."

Todd felt like crying, not from sorrow, but from pure emotion. But he had no tears left. His eyes were dry, like kindling. He knew he had to tell her something—now, while he could still talk. "I'm glad I finally got to meet the real Lila," he choked out, "though I wish we could have reached this level without having to die together."

Lila gazed into his face. Her eyes were large and frightened, but she was smiling bravely. Todd smiled back. She really was beautiful, even with ashes in her hair and dirt on her face. He leaned forward to kiss her, knowing it would be his very last kiss.

Ken stood by Olivia's side, along with the EMT and some of the search-and-rescue specialists as they worked together to toss aside the ceiling beam. Ken braced himself, keeping his eyes on Olivia's face. He remembered how badly it had hurt her earlier when he nudged the beam even a fraction of an inch to one side. This time she didn't move or scream. She didn't even moan.

Fire raged around the group. They still had to

move the refrigerator. The rescue worker's coppery hair reflected the fire's glow as he set up a piece of equipment that reminded Ken of a heavy-duty tire jack. After a short struggle, they lifted the refrigerator and pushed it out of the way.

Olivia still hadn't stirred, but her face was relaxed and peaceful. That had to be a good sign, Ken thought. He hated to see her in pain. He took her cold hand in his as the EMT felt her throat for a pulse. "She's all right," Ken told the man frantically. "She must be all right. Hurry! We have to move her. Get her out before the fire—"

The man shook his head. "I'm sorry," he said softly. "We reached her too late."

"You can't just leave her here to die!" Ken screamed. "There has to be something you can do!"

The EMT took hold of Ken's arm. "She's already gone, son."

"No!" Ken cried. "I won't accept that. You didn't try CPR. You didn't give her an IV. You have to save her!"

The rescuer shook his head. "It's a tragedy, but there's nothing more we can do."

Ken shook his head, staring wildly at the red-headed firefighter, at the EMT . . . at Olivia. "No!" he screamed. "I won't accept that!" He wanted to take her in his arms, kiss her forehead, and will her to open her eyes and prove to them that she was fine.

The man held him back. "You did everything you could for her, Ken. You did a lot more than most people would have."

"Help me lift her!" Ken insisted, barely listening to what they were saying. "We have to carry her out of here. You have more equipment in your truck. You can revive her—"

The EMT shook his head. "I doubt she ever had a chance. Her internal injuries were too extensive. I'm surprised she lasted as long as she did."

"She must have been one brave girl," said the tall blond woman.

"She is!" Ken screamed. "She's the bravest person I know. Don't talk about her in the past tense!"

The red-haired man grabbed him by both shoulders. "Ken, you have to accept what we're telling you. Olivia is dead."

Olivia is dead. Ken fell to his knees and buried his face in her shoulder, trembling with shock and agony. Her neck felt cold against his face, and he began to sob—harsh, wrenching sobs that stabbed through his body and emptied his heart, leaving a hollow core inside him filled only with pain.

How could Olivia be dead? She was Freeverse, his poet and artist—wild and free. She was his soul mate. And his soul. And she was supposed to have waited for him.

Tears rolled down Lila's face as Todd leaned in to kiss her. Her heart raced with a muddled mix of fear and excitement. This was it. The last time she would feel another pair of lips touch her own. And it was Todd. Todd Wilkins—

Suddenly there was a loud snapping sound, and Todd broke away, looking wildly up at the door. The corner had been pulled away like a tin can and a man's face appeared in the jagged hole.

"Come on! Let's get you two out of here!"

Lila could hardly breathe. But she didn't know if it was smoke or elation that caught in her throat. She and Todd scrambled out of the bathtub, raced to the door, and threw themselves through the opening the firefighter had cut with his axe.

"How did you know?" Todd choked out.

"We thought we heard a girl's scream," he said. "But it took me a while to locate you."

An enormous roar burst out behind them. Lila jumped. The firefighter, a muscular, red-haired man, herded them away from the bathroom door.

Lila glanced back over her shoulder through the broken door. The entire room had erupted into billowing flames. Another ten seconds and the rescue effort would have come too late.

A few minutes later Lila couldn't believe she was outside the house, in relative safety. She was standing with Todd and the firefighter in the front yard of what had been the Wakefield house. Plumes of flame still rose from the back, but three hook-and-ladder trucks and two ambulances were parked in the street, along with a smaller rescue vehicle. Firefighters were running back and forth, dragging hoses and equipment not only to the Wakefield yard, but to several others in the neighborhood.

Suddenly Lila realized the sun was rising. "It's morning," she said to Todd, incredulous. For the first time since the earthquake, she was filled with hope. "The night's over."

Todd nodded wordlessly, watching the workers as they tried to control the fires. By the light of the sunrise, Lila began to notice the damage to the surrounding houses. She shuddered, thinking of Fowler Crest. Her hand flew to her mouth. "I have to get home!"

She looked at Todd, hoping he would offer to go with her. He opened his mouth to speak, and she squeezed his hand. But he turned to the fire-fighter instead.

"I want to help," he said to the man. "If the whole town is like this, you'll need all the volunteers you can get."

Lila sighed as the man accepted Todd's offer. He grabbed his radio and spoke to the rest of his team, who were apparently still inside the house, pulling out the body of someone who hadn't made it. The thought made Lila feel sick. That could have been her and Todd. But fear for her parents was beginning to overwhelm her.

A minute later Todd and the firefighter were running to the rescue truck. As Todd climbed in he glanced back in her direction with an expression she couldn't identify. As the truck pulled away with Todd inside it, she was barraged by a mix of bewildering emotions. He'd left so quickly, before they'd had a chance to sort out any of it.

It's only Todd, she told herself. *There's nothing between us. We can't even stand each other.* But watching the truck disappear down Calico Drive, she suddenly felt completely lost and alone.

Ken was bending over Olivia's cold body, crying as he'd never cried before. More firefighters had arrived at some point, and they bustled around him, working to extinguish the fire. But it was already under control near him, and they kept a respectful distance.

"What's that?" Ken heard the tall woman from the rescue team saying.

"It looks like Ken," said the EMT in a tone that sounded like awe.

Something in their voices attracted his attention. He turned to face the two of them, his face dripping tears. They were pulling something flat and square from a mound of debris.

He gasped when the woman held it up. It was a painting—completely undamaged, even in the midst of so much destruction. It was a head-and-shoulders view of Ken, with a background of lush green leaves and kaleidoscopic flowers. His heart skipped a beat. It was the portrait Olivia had redone for him, to put in the school art show.

The woman seemed to be examining one corner of the painting. When she looked down at Ken, tears glittered in her eyes.

"It doesn't have a regular signature," she told him. "It just says, 'With love forever, Olivia.'"

*   *   *

Elizabeth slid back into consciousness and blearily stared up into the face of a handsome stranger. She didn't know him . . . did she? He was about her age, or a little older. His hair was dark. She wanted to ask if he'd rescued her, but her tongue wasn't working. Terrible pain still jangled her entire body, and her mind seemed scrambled. Suddenly she remembered something.

"Enid," she managed to whisper.

The hovering face nodded. "Your friend is fine," his voice said. It was a nice voice, smooth and kind. "You're going to be fine too."

Elizabeth wanted to ask about so many things. Devon had deserted her. She needed to know why. She felt grief, terrible grief, and she knew with sudden clarity that it had something to do with Jessica. She tried to open her mouth, to ask about her sister. It wasn't dark anymore. But her mind was already sliding back into a different kind of darkness, a fuzzy darkness. Like static on a television screen.

"Don't try to talk right now," the voice said. She couldn't see the face anymore. She couldn't see anything but the static.

Jessica sat at the top of the crevasse, motionless except for a trembling she couldn't control. Tears streamed down her face, but Jessica couldn't move, couldn't make a sound. Off to the side somewhere, she heard the sound of retching. It took several minutes for the cause to register in her deadened mind. Bryan was throwing up. She listened to his anguished sobs. He kept crying out Alyssa's name.

Her mind flashed back to that terrible, dark place. Her fingers had grazed the small white hand. Only a few more inches, and she could have grabbed her. She should have worked faster to come up with a plan. She should have stretched her arm just a little bit farther, no matter how badly it strained. A young girl had just died. A family had been devastated. And Jessica had nobody to blame but herself.

The earthquake is over, but the tremors will touch Jessica and Elizabeth's lives in ways they could never have imagined. Will the Wakefield twins and their friends find the strength to go on in a devastated and unfamiliar Sweet Valley? Find out in the next Sweet Valley High Special, **AFTERSHOCK,** *coming next month to a bookstore near you!*

Bantam Books in the Sweet Valley High series
Ask your bookseller for the books you have missed

Surf's Up at Sweet Valley

Francine Pascal's
SWEET VALLEY

Sneak Peeks • Hot News • Meet Francine Pascal • Mailing List • Bookshelf

Check out **Sweet Valley Online** when you're surfing the Internet!
It is *the* place to get the scoop on what's happening with your
favorite twins, Jessica and Elizabeth Wakefield, and the gang at
Sweet Valley. The official site features:

Sneak Peeks
Be the first to know all the juicy details of upcoming books!

Hot News
All the latest and greatest Sweet Valley news including
special promotions and contests.

Meet Francine Pascal
Find out about Sweet Valley's creator and send her a letter by e-mail!

Mailing List
Sign up for Sweet Valley e-mail updates and give us your feedback!

Bookshelf
A handy reference to the World of Sweet Valley.

❤ ★ ❤

Check out Sweet Valley Online today!

http://www.sweetvalley.com

Earthquake Rocks
Sweet Valley!!!

Twin sisters **Jessica** and **Elizabeth Wakefield** have been ripped apart in the chaos following a devastating earthquake.

As they search for each other amidst the rubble, tragedy surrounds them. **Enid Rollins** clings to life by a thread, and **Steven Wakefield,** their brother, risks his life to help his one true love. Most frightening of all, **Todd, Lila, Ken,** and **Olivia** are missing and presumed dead.

Can Jessica and Elizabeth find their friends before it's too late?

Look for these special editions on sale in October and November 1998!

And don't miss a totally new Sweet Valley—New Attitude, New Look, New Everything. SVH: Senior Year coming in January 1999!

BFYR 184